"Come sit by me on the couch," Anne said.

Max eyed her warily. "I don't think so." He met her gaze. "What do you think you're doing, Anne?"

Exasperated, she let out a puff of air and rose to her feet. "I'm trying to seduce you, and since it's perfectly obvious that I'm bad at it, the least you could do is pretend not to notice."

He had started laughing with her first words, and by the time she finished, he was holding her in his arms, rocking them both with his laughter. "Poor baby," he said, still chuckling against her neck. "Want me to teach you?"

"Yes, please," she said quickly. "It's been so long—"

"How long has it been?" Max demanded. "Months? Years?"

"Months . . . years," she said quietly. "It doesn't matter."

He whistled softly and turned his head to stare at the fireplace. She picked up his hand and brushed his palm with her lips. When she lingered, he sucked in a sharp breath. "Lady, you don't need any lessons. Do you know what I was thinking? That you're either the only human in history without physical needs. Or . . ." He curved his hand around her neck and slowly drew her toward him. "Or you're a time bomb waiting to explode."

She smiled. "Tick . . . tick . . . tick . . ."

WHAT ARE *LOVESWEPT* ROMANCES?

They are stories of true romance and touching emotion. We believe those two very important ingredients are constants in our highly sensual and very believable stories in the *LOVESWEPT* line. Our goal is to give you, the reader, stories of consistently high quality that may sometimes make you laugh, sometimes make you cry, but are always fresh and creative and contain many delightful surprises within their pages.

Most romance fans read an enormous number of books. Those they truly love, they keep. Others may be traded with friends and soon forgotten. We hope that each *LOVESWEPT* romance will be a treasure—a "keeper." We will always try to publish

LOVE STORIES YOU'LL NEVER FORGET
BY AUTHORS YOU'LL ALWAYS REMEMBER

The Editors

Billie Green

In Annie's Eyes

BANTAM BOOKS

NEW YORK · TORONTO · LONDON · SYDNEY · AUCKLAND

IN ANNIE'S EYES

A Bantam Book / November 1991

If you would be interested in receiving protective vinyl
covers for your Loveswept books, please write to this address
for information:

Loveswept
Bantam Books
P.O. Box 985
Hicksville, NY 11802

ISBN 0-553-44157-4

Published simultaneously in the United States and Canada

Bantam Books are published by Bantam Books, a division
of Bantam Doubleday Dell Publishing Group, Inc. Its trademark, consisting of the words "Bantam Books" and the
portrayal of a rooster, is Registered in U.S. Patent and
Trademark Office and in other countries. Marca Registrada.
Bantam Books, 666 Fifth Avenue, New York, New York
10103.

PRINTED IN THE UNITED STATES OF AMERICA

OPM   0 9 8 7 6 5 4 3 2 1

To Jim and Barbara, for showing me how warm and abiding love can be.

One

When it happened, when Max finally found her again, he was walking down an ordinary street, on a cloudy but ordinary day in mid-March. And as little as he liked admitting it, there was probably nothing out of the ordinary about his restless, inward-turning thoughts or the fact that lately he had begun to suspect that Sartre might have been on to something when he called man a useless passion.

The street, the day, the mood—all were ordinary; then the sun broke through the clouds, and on this ordinary day, on this ordinary street, he saw her.

And that was where ordinary stopped.

Even after eleven years, even with a four-lane, traffic-filled street between them, he had no trouble recognizing her. He knew her instantly and without a doubt. Her hairstyle—pulled to

the back of her head in a smooth twist—
was unfamiliar, but the rose-gold hair was the
same. The sober gray business suit was more
sophisticated—more expensive—than the clothes
she had worn in the past, but she still had that
unmistakable, unnameable quality about her.
Something in her delicate features, something
about the way she moved, caught and held the
eye, as though she were not quite real, a delicate
fairy-child who had strayed away from a softer,
more serene world.

Now, as Max watched from across the street,
he saw her speak to the man walking beside her,
and when her companion looked down at her,
when Max saw the man smile at her, a wave of
something close to nausea swept over him.

Max had spent a significant amount of time in
the past eleven years wondering how he would
feel if he ever saw her again, and now, as he
heard a blaring horn—an indignant warning
from the car he had almost stepped in front
of—he knew. Nothing had changed. She could
still move him. She could still make him act
without thinking.

Stepping back onto the sidewalk, he shoved
clenched fists into the pockets of his leather
jacket. Seeing her, feeling all the old feelings—as
new, as immediate, as twisted and tangled and
white hot, as they had been eleven years ago—
left him shaking all over.

Get a grip, he told himself as he forced air into
tight lungs. He needed time to think.

Max had waited a long time for this chance. A

long, hard, hellish time. He could wait a little while longer.

"Cliff . . . Cliff?" Anne slowed down to wait for her employer and friend. "What are you looking at?"

"What? Oh nothing, just that guy over—"

"Where?" She glanced across the street. Occupying the opposite corner was a teenage boy with orange hair that had been moussed, gelled, and spritzed into a flaring headdress. "It's life, Captain Kirk, but not as we know it," she murmured, her gray eyes widening in amazement.

"Not him," Cliff said. "He's gone now, but he started to cross the— Have you ever lived in San Antonio?"

Anne stopped walking and cut her eyes toward the man beside her. "Am I supposed to buy a vowel or something? I don't—Oh, I see." Her lips twitched in a slight smile. "You're trying to delve into my shady past again. No, I've never lived in San Antonio." Glancing at her watch, she added, "We're going to be late. I'm afraid that shortcut was a mistake." The last words were thrown over her shoulder as she ran up the wide steps of a pink-granite office building.

In the elevator Cliff said, "Ever vacation here?"

"No. No vacation, no weekend trips. I've never even passed through here on my way to somewhere else. This is my very first visit to San Antonio." She raised her gaze to him in gentle amusement. "And if the man you saw was someone from my past, he was probably trying to get across the street so he could strangle me."

The doors slid open on the fifth floor and several people stepped out of the elevator. After a moment, without looking at her, Cliff said, "You were maybe a Russian spy before I met you?"

Anne's breath caught somewhere between a cough and a laugh. "No," she said finally, "nothing so internationally important, but there were times—" She broke off, and exhaled slowly. "Please, can we change the subject? You've got to stop trying to pair me off with every man you see."

His lips twisted in a wry, almost sad smile. "I just don't like seeing you alone."

"Then set a better example for me," she said quietly. "It's been over four years since Paula died."

Cliff Wariner and his wife had only recently celebrated their twentieth anniversary when Paula died as a result of a stroke. And although Cliff was constantly nagging Anne about her single state, he hadn't had so much as a casual date in the past four years.

Seeing the melancholy that lingered in her friend's eyes, Anne jostled his arm. "Hey, we're doing okay, just the way we are. Two gung-ho, career-minded, executive types. Right?"

After a moment he smiled, a real smile this time. "Right."

"And we're going to go in there and sell this project. Right?" When he didn't respond, she repeated, "Right?"

As the doors slid open again, he straightened

his shoulders and moved forward. "We're going to give it one hell of a try."

Hector Sanchez, president and majority stock-holder of Alto Tool and Die, knew why Anne and Cliff were there to see him. Cliff had spoken to the man several times over the phone. Today was merely the final pitch. Today Emily, the small town where both Cliff and Anne lived, would either be saved or the quest would go on.

In the small, sparsely furnished office, Sanchez leaned back in a battered leather chair and studied the two people who occupied the chairs on the opposite side of his desk. "I can see how the closing of the steel mill could have generated a decline in the local economy around"—he glanced down at the paper in his hand—"Emily. Good name for a town. Friendly." He paused to light a cigarette. "And don't think I don't sympathize. I do. I genuinely do. But you gotta know there are a lot of little towns suffering—"

"A decline in the local economy?" Anne repeated, her soft voice incredulous. "That's a nice phrase, Mr. Sanchez. Nice and distant. But it doesn't even begin to cover the situation we've got in Emily. People, *good people*, are hurting. You can't pigeonhole—"

"Anne," Cliff broke in, his voice calm but firm.

Biting her lower lip, she leaned back in her chair. Cliff was right. They hadn't come here to make an emotional appeal. They were in Hector Sanchez's office to convince him that building one of his factories in Emily would be good for Alto Tool and Die.

The only problem was that for Anne it *was*

emotional. The people in Emily didn't care about charts and statistics, and they didn't understand economic catchphrases. They only knew that when the steel mill closed, almost a third of their population had been thrown out of work. And that left them with only two choices: pack up and leave or find a company to replace the mill. For most of them, leaving wasn't an option. Emily was home. Emily was where they belonged. It was a place of porch swings and fried chicken, dancing to country music at the Longhorn Palace on Saturday nights and washing the car after church on Sunday. It was a place where you cared about your neighbor and took his troubles as your own.

The job Anne and Cliff had accepted, this tracking down of a business that would employ as many people as the steel mill had, should have been handled by the mayor or one of the other city officials, but neither Mayor Hilley nor the councilmen were politicians. They were farmers and veterinarians and construction workers.

"No one's going to listen to us," they told Cliff, "but you talk their language. You're our last best hope."

Cliff, the owner of a small but successful chain of computer stores, was Emily's leading citizen, and the people there believed in him totally. The way Cliff saw it, that kind of trust left him no choice. He had to do everything in his power to help pull his hometown through this crisis. Which was why in the past few weeks Anne and Cliff had flown all over the country, meeting the COOs and CEOs and plain old presidents, giving the same presentation to identically ambivalent faces, trying to convince someone—*anyone*—that a small town in south-central Texas would be the perfect site for expansion or relocation. And that was why they were in San Antonio today, talking to a man who obviously wished he had never invited them to sit down.

While Cliff gave Sanchez an overview of the generous concessions the town was willing to make—roads built, land leveled, utilities and real estate discounted, Sanchez scribbled idly on a piece of paper. And when Anne took over to tell him about the work force in Emily, about the loyalty that was ingrained in the people, Sanchez held his hands in a steeple in front of his face and played finger games. By the time Hector Sanchez ended the meeting, wishing them luck in their venture, Anne wanted to do something nasty and irreversible to his knee-caps.

Two hours later, as they drove away from Emily's small airstrip, neither Anne nor Cliff had mentioned the disappointing results of the meeting. Slipping on her reading glasses, Anne thumbed through the lists she and Cliff had put together a month earlier, lists that dwindled daily.

"So next week it's Houston again," she said as she checked a small appointment book. "What's the name of that textile outfit? Jayco, Dayglo—no, that's paint. Anyway, don't you think we could push them a little and get that meeting—"

"He had his mind made up before we ever walked through the door," Cliff broke in, his voice flat with dejection.

"Cliff—"

"No pep talks, Anne. I won't give up, you know that, but . . . I can handle when we get a turndown based on solid facts, when there are sound reasons for the rejection of our proposal, but Sanchez didn't even listen." He shook his head. "Never mind. Next time we'll make them listen."

He relaxed his grip on the steering wheel and shot a glance in her direction. "What you said in the elevator, I mean about that man crossing the street to strangle you, you didn't really mean that . . . did you?"

Pulling off her glasses, she placed them on the dash and avoided Cliff's eyes as she began to massage the bridge of her nose.

After a moment of silence he said, "It's not just curiosity, Anne. I know I shouldn't, but I worry about you."

"Come on, Cliff." She shifted her position restlessly. "Don't you think I know? You're one of the kindest, most generous men I've ever known. And I know I owe you a—"

"Don't talk to me about owing," he said, his voice suddenly harsh. "I may have given you a good job, but in return I got the best assistant I've ever had. You take care of things before I even know they need taking care of. And if you hadn't been there for me when Paula died—" He broke off and cleared his throat. "We won't talk about owing. And we won't talk about your past, if that's the way you want it."

"There's nothing mysterious or even particularly interesting about my past," she said quietly. "Everyone has failures. We all have things we did when we were young . . . foolish things, things we regret with all our heart and would rather not remember."

"I have a feeling we're talking about something a little more important than sneaking a smoke behind the barn."

Smiling at his persistence, she said, "That's a country thing. In the city we sneaked cigarettes in the alley. The truth is, I simply don't have a good history with men. Now, there's an understatement," she added in a wry tone. "They always want something that I don't know how to give, and their need always takes me by surprise. I'll go along thinking some man is a really good friend, then suddenly I get hit in the face with an assortment of sexual-slash-emotional demands." She shook her head slowly. "I know that the fault is in me. I should be better at reading people, and I feel guilty about it, believe me, but I don't know how to change. So the only solution was for me to avoid close relationships. It's as simple as that."

"There's more. You know it and I know it," he said firmly as he turned the car off the highway onto a crushed-rock lane that ran beside a wide, shallow river. "But I'll drop the subject . . . for now."

Giving a soft laugh, Anne leaned back and allowed her tense shoulders to relax. As they drove along the narrow road, she caught an occasional glimpse in the distance, through the cottonwóods and willows, of the house that had been her home for the past four years and, as always, she felt a strange little shiver of pleasure shake through her at the sight. Built of the same rock that formed the riverbed, the house and the landscape around it looked soft and gentle, like a watercolor painting. But there were times, when the rays of a setting sun struck it at just the right angle, that the scene came alive with dazzling color so splendid, it hurt the eyes to look. And all of it, the serenity and the fire, belonged to Anne. It was the home she had always longed for.

Moments later, as she got out of the car, Cliff leaned across the seat and said, "How about let's take tomorrow morning off? We've both been working too— Oh, come on, Anne. You don't have to give me that I-should-be-mothering-him look. I'm not getting old and I'm not getting discouraged. I'm supposed to be in semiretirement, for Pete's sake. Do you know how long it's been since I've gone fishing? I just want to go fishing."

Cliff didn't actually fish; he simply sat in the middle of the river in his leaky old boat and spent hours looking at birds and clouds and sky.

Hiding her smile, she said, "Stop whining. You don't need my permission to go fishing."

As soon as his big white Cadillac disappeared around the bend, she walked inside, stripping off her clothes as she headed for the bathroom.

She showered quickly, unwilling to linger, afraid she would miss sunset on the river. Her need for the river was acute. Vital. She needed it to ease her out of this restless, pressured mood.

After slipping on a terry-cloth robe, she made a pot of coffee and took a cup with her out to the small stone terrace that overlooked the river. As the setting sun threw long shadows across the river, she settled down in a wide wicker chair and drank her coffee.

Slow, quiet moments passed as she waited for the tension to drain, as she waited for the peace to find her. But tonight peace stayed away.

She shouldn't have talked to Cliff about the past, she realized. Not even that little bit. Because now the past wouldn't go away. The feel of it tingled on her fingertips, and the taste of it lay on her tongue.

"Weiden Street," she whispered.

Anne had been five years old when she and her mother moved to East Dallas, to the house on Weiden Street, and the move to a real neighborhood thrilled her. She had never had her very own bedroom before; she had never had her very own *bed*. In the apartment she had slept on the couch or, when the couch wasn't available, on a pallet on the floor. Another thing she had never had was a yard. Her playground had always been a cement parking lot, in and around dumpsters. Their new home not only had a real yard—a tiny piece of land with brittle-dry grass— it also had flowers and trees. For a too-small, too-wise five-year-old, it was paradise.

Anne had only ever had one parent. Her mother

never got around to explaining where, or even who, her father was, leaving Anne to assume he simply didn't exist. So Anne was used to taking care of herself during the day while her mother worked, sometimes at night as well. She didn't mind being left alone. Not really. She had her books, her imagination, and unlimited freedom. Most of the time those were enough.

When they had been in the new house for two weeks, after exploring every inch of her new yard, checking out every dandelion, staking claim to every limb in the rosebush that grew outside her bedroom window, Anne decided it was time to see what the rest of Weiden Street was like.

It was a beautiful day, warm and bright, and she hadn't gone half a block before she saw the little girls playing, two of them, their hair pulled up into neat ponytails as they sat on a blanket in the shade of a flowering tree.

Anne stood quietly on the sidewalk and watched them as they spoke in grown-up voices to their baby dolls. She had always loved watching children at play. It was better than television.

"Do you have a baby?" one of the little girls called to her.

When Anne shook her head slowly from side to side, the girl held up a balding doll. "You can play with Lisa Sue if you want to."

Anne stood where she was for a moment, then with cautious steps she began to move closer, glancing warily at the house, at the big windows there. But no one was watching. Maybe it would be all right this time.

Folding her legs beneath her, she sat on the far corner of the blanket and cradled the doll in her arms, stroking the hair that had once been silky but was now falling out in stiff clumps. She didn't touch anything else, not the tiny diapers or the plastic baby bottles, unless it was offered to her. And she didn't talk. She did what she always did. She listened, avidly taking in the girls' giggling chatter, their friendly bickering.

Too soon she heard a screen door slam, and suddenly three older boys were standing beside the blanket, shouting at her. "Go home," they said. "Our mother says for you to go home and play in your own yard. You're not allowed to play with our sisters," the boys told her.

Anne didn't argue. Placing Lisa Sue carefully on the blanket, she stood up, and without looking at any of them, she turned to go. The boys were still yelling at her, louder now, as though they were disappointed that she wasn't arguing, as though shouting at her gave them power over her.

Anne had been yelled at before, and she understood that her silence always made it worse, but she didn't know how else to react. Something inside made her raise her chin and hide her fear. Something made her move with unhurried dignity.

It was only when a small stone struck her cheek that she began to run. And as she had known they would, the boys chased her, calling out names, ugly names that Anne had heard many times in the past. She ran as fast as she could, but not from the boys and their rocks. She was trying to outrun the words.

When she reached the corner and paused, panicking because she didn't know which way to go, she felt someone grab her from behind. The thing inside her, the unknown quantity that made her raise her chin, now made her fight with everything that was in her. She kicked and scratched and bit, her breath coming in harsh gasps.

"Calm down, kid," a voice said in her ear. "Stop kicking, for Pete's sake. I'm one of the good guys."

Before she could respond, Anne heard the noisy approach of her persecutors. She was released abruptly, and when she turned around, she saw a boy older than herself, maybe ten, with blond hair and laughing brown eyes throwing wild punches at the three who had chased her. It was one against three, but that was a fact the other boys didn't seem to realize, because seconds later they scattered and fled.

After shaking his fist at them in a dramatic gesture, the blond boy walked back to where she stood. "You okay, kid?" he asked as he squatted beside her. "What happened to your face?"

When he gently touched her cheek, Anne leaned against him. She didn't cry. She never cried. But even though she was no longer afraid, she couldn't stop shaking as he stroked her tangled hair, murmuring, "Poor little squirt, you poor little squirt. What's your name?"

"Annie. Annie Sea—"

"What's up?"

This was a new voice, and Anne looked up to find a girl, nearer her own age but tall and thin and dark, standing beside them.

"Her name's Annie. Old fatso and his zit-faced brothers were chasing her," the blond boy explained as he straightened away from Anne.

"The stupid snots. What'd you do to them, kid?" the dark girl asked.

Anne stared down at her sandaled feet. "They didn't want me to play with the dolls," she said softly.

But Anne knew it wasn't the dolls. She had always known there was something wrong with her, something so bad that other children, good little children, were not allowed to play with her. And although she had hoped it would be different on Weiden Street, she hadn't counted on it.

"Hey, you don't want to play with dumb old dolls anyway," the boy said. "That's sissy stuff. You can play with me and Ellie from now on."

"Sure . . . sure you can," the girl named Ellie said, then shot a look at the boy. "But what'll we do with her, Max? She looks like a baby ballerina or something. How's she going to help us fight off the bad guys?"

Max glanced down at Anne. "She's a pretty good fighter, but we don't need another swordsman. What we need is a queen who's trapped in the tower. We can put her up in the chinaberry tree. Then we'll really have something to rescue."

After a moment Ellie shrugged. "Okay, but she needs some stuff. A long dress and a—"

"They won't let you play with me," Anne blurted

out. She didn't want to tell them, but she knew they would find out sooner or later.

"Who won't?" Max asked, his expression growing belligerent. "Old fatso and his stinkin' brothers?"

Anne shook her head in short, jerky movements. "Your mother. Or hers. They won't let you," she said, her throat tight, her voice intense. "They just won't."

"Why?" Ellie asked, looking really interested for the first time. "Have you got something contagious?"

Anne looked from one to the other, embarrassed that she didn't understand the word.

"She means are you sick and is it catching," Max explained.

Anne considered the question and finally, with a sigh, she whispered, "Maybe."

Ellie backed away slightly, but not Max. He put his hand on Anne's shoulder and said, "We'd better get you home, then. Where do you live?"

She pointed down the street. "201. 201 Weiden Street," she said, proud that she had memorized her new address.

An awkward silence fell around her. Glancing up, Anne found Max and Ellie staring at each other over her head.

Moments later Ellie whistled softly through her teeth. "Her mother's the one who—" She broke off and her features were softer as she leaned down to hug Anne.

Max's fingers clenched into fists, and he swung away. "Rotten bastards. Dirty, rotten bastards. That's why nobody's allowed to play with her."

With an abrupt movement he turned back and squatted beside her again, one hand firmly on her shoulder. "You got us now, squirt. You hear? You got me and Ellie. That's all you need."

She wanted desperately to believe him. For the few moments that she had leaned against him, as he had stroked her hair and talked gently to her, Anne had felt safe. For the first time in her life she had felt completely safe.

Surprisingly the feeling of security had stayed with her. Ellie and Max, for reasons Anne didn't understand until much later, were allowed to play with her, and as the years passed, the trio stayed together. They built their own world and raised each other, forming bonds that were stronger than blood.

"And then it was gone," Anne whispered as she rested her chin on her knees. "All gone."

When the darkness of night began to fade, when sunlight slowly spread through the trees across the river, Anne was still sitting in the wicker chair, caught up in things of yesterday, unable to go back and change the past, yet unwilling to let it go. Unwilling to let *him* go.

But of course it wasn't a matter of remembering or not remembering. Nothing was ever that simple. If someone sat down and made a list of the different elements that formed the woman named Anne Seaton, he would be on the list. Heart, lungs, brain, Max . . .

Even now, when she closed her eyes, she could see his face as it had been eleven years ago. And she could see it changing, growing older and harder. She could see his features, twisted with anger as he shouted the hateful words at her.

"You're a whore just like your mother!"

Her eyes flew open, and she held tightly clenched fingers to her chest, trying to catch her breath. It didn't happen, she told herself. *It didn't happen.* He never looked like that. He never said those words.

But he would. If she ever saw him again, he would.

Two

On her knees in the backyard, Anne took bright-orange impatiens from plastic pots and transferred them to her garden. The small plot that surrounded the terrace was filled, for the most part, with greenery—ferns, grasses, and exotic succulents—but she liked to see an occasional splash of color mixed in.

As she worked, she felt the sun on her bare shoulders, and now and then she turned her head toward the river. She wasn't looking for anything. She simply liked to see the water slipping over and around the rocks. She liked knowing the same sun that warmed her flesh was adding sparkle to the river.

Minutes later when she heard her name being called, Anne shouted, "Come on around. I'm in the garden."

Still on her knees, she swung around to catch

the tiny, raven-haired boy who hurled himself at her, laughing with him as his weight knocked her down on her backside.

"Petey, for heaven's sake, don't kill her."

Carly Angelo, Petey's mother and Anne's best friend, issued the casual, offhand command as she flopped down on a padded lounger.

"Anne, oh, Anne." The sad words came from the four-year-old who still clung to her neck.

"Petey, oh, Petey," Anne said, smiling in gentle sympathy. "What's wrong, love?"

"My little shovel got lost."

"Here," she said, picking up her trowel. "Use mine."

"Only while we're here, Petey," his mother warned. "If you take it home, it'll get lost like the other one." She glanced at Anne. "He was burying more treasure in the backyard, so the trowel's probably underground somewhere, along with that awful plastic angel Aunt Josh gave him."

As Carly spoke, she shifted her position, her movements languid and unconsciously sensual. The redhead was something of a legend in Emily. At seventeen she had left town to seek fame and fortune in Hollywood. Several commercials and an ill-fated situation comedy later, Carly came home carrying one shabby suitcase and an infant son. Offering no explanations, she moved in with her widowed mother and took a job serving drinks at the Longhorn, a club that Cliff owned.

Anne had decided long ago that Carly's flashy clothes and blunt way of speaking were a form of self-defense. The redhead knew she was the cause of gossip and willfully played the role of bad girl to the hilt.

"I envy you, you know," Anne said as she gazed at the small figure squatting in her garden, and concentrating with fierce intensity on each scoop of dirt.

"I'll sell him to you. Marked down to half price, today only."

"I wish," Anne said, knowing Carly would fight with her bare hands anyone who tried to take her son.

"He was worried because we didn't ask you to go to the carnival with us. He said you didn't have a little boy to take you. He's in love with you," Carly added with a resigned sigh, "just like every other male in town."

Dusting off her hands, Anne rose to her feet. "They're not in love with me. They feel sorry for me because I'm an ignorant city girl."

"Yeah, right." Carly was openly skeptical. "For heaven's sake, sit down. You know, I've never seen you do nothing. I mean, just lie back and do absolutely nothing. You've got this sweet, serene look, but you never stop moving."

Giving a soft laugh, Anne took the matching lounger, but instead of lying back, she wrapped her arms around her knees. "Maybe I'm afraid if I ever stop, I might look around my life and find out there's nothing there."

Carly drew back her head in surprise. "What's this? That sounded a lot like cynicism, my dear. In fact it sounded a lot like me. Is my bad attitude rubbing off on you?"

Frowning, Anne shook her head. "I don't know why I said that," she said. "I love my life. I'm so lucky, luckier than I deserve, I sometimes think."

"Now, that sounds more like our humble little Saint Anne." After a slight pause Carly said, "Is there something going on between you and Cliff?"

The abrupt change of subject caught Anne off guard. "Why on earth would you ask something like that? You know how I feel about Cliff. In a better world, in a fair and impartial world, Cliff would have been my father. He's the kind of man I always dreamed my father would be." She made a wry face. "Of course I had to create some pretty fantastic reasons why a man so kind and caring would leave me and never—not once in my whole life—bother to get in touch."

Disliking the bitterness she heard in her own voice, Anne shook the feeling away and repeated, "Why did you ask something like that?"

"I don't know, it's just that ever since the trip to San Antonio you've been weird. I thought maybe something had happened between you two."

Carly sounded casual, too casual, and Anne's eyes widened as an idea nudged her. "You're in love with Cliff," she said slowly. "Why didn't I see it? Carly, that's so exciting. You're perfect for—"

"Anne, stop it!" Carly snapped, her features harsh. "You know damn well I don't believe in that kind of thing. I love Petey. I love Mama. I love my cashmere coat and my new blue dress. But what you're talking about—" She broke off, and drew in a steadying breath. "It's like Big-foot. Until I can reach out and touch that sucker myself, I refuse to believe it exists."

When Anne opened her mouth to protest, Carly said, "Stop trying to distract me. If it isn't about Cliff, what happened to you in San Antonio? You're different. Like your body is here, but you're seeing, you're *feeling*, some other place or time."

Anne glanced away from her friend toward the river. *Another place, another time.* What did Carly see in her face? Not once in the three days since their trip to San Antonio had Anne allowed the past to catch hold of her again, yet Carly still saw it, felt its presence in her.

"Aren't you happy here?" Carly asked quietly.

Swinging her head around sharply, Anne stared at the other woman. "Are you out of your mind? Emily . . . this town is my home now. The people here are my family. You don't know what it means—"

She stopped and shook her head. Until four years ago Anne had never heard of Emily. When Cliff decided to semiretire, when he decided to return to the town where he was born and raised, he had asked her to come with him and continue in her job as his assistant. Anne hadn't hesitated. She had no family to leave behind, nothing to hold her in Houston. And the thought of being an outsider in a small, closed community hadn't bothered her. She had been alone for a long time. She was used to it.

But the people in Emily hadn't acted the way they were supposed to act. They hadn't looked at her with suspicion. They hadn't inspected her with superior, withdrawn interest. They had accepted her immediately and completely.

"From the very first day it was like I belonged," Anne said, her voice soft with awe. "Like I had been away for a long time and had finally come home. You were born here, and you take that kind of thing for granted. You knew they would welcome you back, but to me it's . . . it's like a miracle."

"They welcomed me back, all right," Carly said with heavy sarcasm. "And they're nice when I meet them on the street or serve them a drink. Then they go home and rip me apart over their pot roast and snap beans. 'That Carly always was a wild one. I knew she'd come to no good, bringing home her little sooty-headed mistake like that, not a husband or wedding ring in sight.'"

"Carly!"

"Sorry." The tension in the redhead's face eased a little. "That sounded ugly, didn't it? You're right, I'm lucky. They may talk about me, but they all love Petey. I can't ask for more than that."

"What's not to love?" Anne said, grinning. "I wonder how many impatiens I have left?"

"It's your own fault. You shouldn't have turned him loose with that trowel."

Anne glanced around, feeling suddenly restless. Carly was right. She couldn't be still for long. "I guess I should make a move soon . . . get ready for the meeting tonight."

Cliff had called a strategy meeting for eight

that evening. They would get together with the mayor and councilmen at the Longhorn. Due to a small but messy water leak, the club had been closed for several days, which meant the group would be able to talk privately in an informal atmosphere. Cliff and Anne would use the time to bring the council members up-to-date on the Houston companies they would be approaching on their trip next week.

"Anne." When Anne glanced up to see the redhead studying her, Carly said, "You're not going to tell me what's wrong, are you?"

"Nothing . . . no really, it's nothing. Just a mood. Oh, you know how it is. Spring always brings on those stupid nostalgia binges." She laughed. "You start brooding about the time you had to go to the prom with a short cousin, that kind of thing. Like I said, it's nothing."

"If your memories make you look like that, your past must be as interesting as mine. Maybe we should swap war stories sometime." Rising to her feet, she added, "Come on, Petey mine, time to go. No, leave the lizard. All its friends and relatives are here." She glanced over her shoulder at Anne. "Want to ride to the meeting with me? Frank, bless his grim little heart, volunteered me to serve drinks."

Frank Carter was the bartender at the Longhorn and Carly's boss. "Nice of him," Anne said. "Thanks, I could use some company. See you tonight. 'Bye, Petey," she called as the two disappeared around the corner. She slid off the chaise and returned to her gardening, repairing the damage Petey had caused with the "little shovel."

The cool, damp earth beneath her fingers worked subtly to soothe and comfort her. Even before Anne was old enough to know the difference between a dandelion and a marigold, she had loved working with the green, growing things of the earth, and by the time she was ten, she was using a big stainless steel spoon to transfer pretty weeds into her little garden, along with the wilting daisies and brown-edged irises Max and Ellie salvaged for her from empty houses.

To Anne the makeshift garden was beautiful, weeds and all, but then one day Max began to bring her plants that were different—gloriously flowering plants with lush greenery. She had been beside herself with excitement . . . until he presented her with a set of brand-new, wood-handled gardening tools. That was when Anne finally stopped to ask herself where the gifts were coming from. The flowers he brought to her weren't neglected plants rescued from abandoned yards, nor were they castoffs he had scavenged from the alley behind the local nursery. They were well-tended plants. Healthy. Costly.

Although Max had a job sweeping up at the local pool hall, he gave most of his salary to his aunt for room and board; he rarely even had money for new clothes. There was most certainly no money for anything as frivolous as a hothouse plant. So how had he acquired them?

Almost as soon as the question took form, the

answer—the only possible answer—followed: Max was stealing.

When Anne caught up with him, he was carving his initials into an aged peach tree. At fifteen Max was almost double her height, his body tanned and lean and as hard as whipcord. When he smiled, which he did more often than not back then, there was a flash of uneven teeth, a glimpse of solitary dimple. His dark-blond hair was long, reaching almost to his shoulders, and he wore a faded T-shirt tucked into tight, threadbare jeans. It was a rough, rebellious look, a look that made his Aunt Charlotte cringe. It was a look that even a ten-year-old recognized as unabashedly sensual.

"You took them. The plants and the tools— you took them, didn't you?" Anne's face was set in stubborn lines as she stared up at the boy who had come to mean more to her than anything in life.

Finishing the initials, Max pocketed the knife, then gave her a casual glance. "Drop it, squirt."

"Didn't you?"

"Hey, I thought you liked the stuff I brought you," he hedged, grinning as he leaned against the tree. "You had a fit over that red thing."

"I loved it," she admitted reluctantly. "I loved all of it, but—"

"You think anybody's gonna miss that piddly old stuff? You think they can't just go out and buy some more?"

"I don't care about that," she said with quiet intensity. "It's . . . it's *you*."

"Judas priest, will you stop whining?"

"No, I won't," she said. "I'll whine forever. I'll walk behind you everywhere you go and whine until it drives you crazy. And . . . and I'll cry, Max. You know how you'd hate that."

He studied her face, then made a rough sound of exasperation. "Look around you, squirt. For Pete's sake, you think this is Highland Freakin' Park or something? This is the real world. So I swiped some stuff. Big deal. People take things. It's just another way to get along."

"But see—" She had to swallow hard to keep her voice steady. "Max, people who steal go to jail." She put her hand on his arm, her eyes burning with suppressed emotion. "You have to promise you won't swipe anything else. Because people get caught, and *they go to jail.*"

He swung abruptly away from her earnest gaze. "Dammit, Annie, haven't I told you not to look at me like that? Those eyes of yours could drive a guy crazy. A kid like you has no business with Joan of Arc eyes anyway."

Anne had never head of Joan of Arc, and she didn't know why he was talking about her eyes. She only knew that he still hadn't promised he would stop stealing. "Max?" she whispered.

After a moment he turned back to her, calm and smiling again, showing her the uneven teeth and that solitary dimple as he raised one brow. "You called me a crook, didn't you? Bad move, squirt, really bad move. You know what that means . . . don't you? Well, come on, I'm waiting."

She nodded, seeing nothing out of the way in his demand. "Please accept my most sincere and humble apology, O great and magnificent Max-imilian," she said in a breathless rush. Then she added, "But I'm not going down on my knees, Max, because you *are* stealing. And I don't want you to do it anymore."

Picking up his hand, she laid the callused palm against her cheek. "Please, Max."

The smile had disappeared, and he stared at her for a long time, his expression a complicated mixture of anger and sadness and something that might have been awe.

Finally he gave his head a rough shake and muttered, "You beat everything, you know that?"

So in the end he had given in to her pleas, calling her his conscience. But ethics had never been involved. Always, even at the beginning, Anne had put her feelings for Max above ethics, above the law. She had simply been afraid for him. Afraid he would be caught and sent to jail. She was quite literally terrified that he would leave her.

And now, as she sat on the cool flagstones beside the flower bed, Anne felt the same emotions Carly had sensed in her earlier, that overwhelming connection with other times, other places.

Why did everything have to remind her of Max? she wondered wearily. It wasn't normal, this constant dwelling on the past. It was for this very reason that she didn't date, didn't encourage close relationships with men. Because there was nothing in her present that could compare with, much less overpower, the past.

"God," she whispered, raising her face toward the dwindling light, "I'm tired. I am so tired."

She was tired of *almost* existing. Tired of living in the shadow of life. She wanted children. A laughing little boy like Petey. A delicate-faced little girl. Heaven help her, she wanted a normal life.

Rising to her feet, she dusted off her hands with slow, mechanical movements. It was foolish to sit around feeling sorry for herself. She had chosen this path of her own free will. Eleven years ago she had made the decision that brought her directly to this point, and regretting what couldn't be changed was worse than useless: It wasted emotional energy that she couldn't afford to lose.

In the house Anne showered quickly and dressed in a white blouse and dove-gray wool jumper. After pinning her hair back with a mother-of-pearl clip, she spent the next half hour going over her notes, trying to find something that looked encouraging, something that would give the men at the meeting a little hope for the future.

Unfortunately she was still thumbing through the papers, still searching for that little bit of hope, as she sat beside Carly in the front seat of her friend's battered Dodge.

"Those little round glasses make you look like the schoolmarm on *Little House on the Prairie*," Carly said, then paused. "It isn't going to work, is it? Why should any company build here? There are thousands of towns like Emily. What do we have that the others don't?"

"We have Cliff," Anne said quietly. "And we have people willing to pull together and make sacrifices for the good of the town. In the past few weeks I've heard no said in a dozen different ways. But I have never—not even once, Carly— doubted that we would succeed. It's just a matter of finding the right company."

"I hope to God you're right," Carly said as they pulled into a graveled lot.

The parking lot was located directly in front of a square brick building. At some point in the past someone had painted the bricks a cinnamon brown, but the paint had worn off in large patches, giving the exterior an interesting, mangy-dog look. The sign over the door was supposed to inform those who didn't know that this was the LONGHORN PALACE, but since the sign had been painted at approximately the same time as the building, those who didn't know would think it was the LOGORPLAC. Of course it really didn't matter, because in Emily there weren't any who didn't know.

Cliff's father, Daryl Wariner, had built the Longhorn back in the forties, and when Cliff inherited the place, he didn't even consider renovating. He understood that the Longhorn was an institution in Emily. People liked it just the way it was.

When Anne and Carly walked into the club, only two men were there, both standing behind the gleaming wood-and-brass bar. Frank, the bartender, was short, wiry, and wore an expression of habitual pugnacity. The other man, Frank's younger brother, Leon, was the Longhorn's bouncer cum maintenance man and physically the exact opposite of the bartender. People stayed out of Leon's way, mostly because he stood six-four and weighed two hundred and sixty pounds, and partly because everyone remembered that Leon had spent several years in prison for negligent homicide.

"You sure do look pretty tonight, Miss Anne," Leon said, his voice characteristically soft.

"Thank you, Leon." She smiled, then glanced at Carly. "You want to help me push some of the tables together?"

When Anne began moving chairs away from one of the square tables, both Leon and Frank protested, gently pushing her back so that they could rearrange the tables for her.

"They wouldn't lift a finger for *me*," Carly muttered, "not if all the tables and the freaking roof fell on top of me. Both of them have a stupid crush on you, and I tell you right now, Anne, this is a trend that's beginning to make me nauseous."

Anne grinned at her friend. The redhead liked to complain. The only reason Leon and Frank didn't try to help Carly was because they knew she would be offended at any suggestion of weakness. And given Carly's temper, she wasn't someone you wanted to offend. As Leon had once told Anne, "A guy could get his arm broke that way."

After the tables had been arranged to suit Anne, Carly began distributing little bowls of nuts and pretzels and hard candy around the table—Mayor Hilley couldn't think without hard

candy in his mouth—while Anne arranged cop-
ies of her report at each place, then checked to
make sure her tape recorder was working. Anne
never took notes at these meetings because the
councilmen were in the habit of all talking at
once, each trying to shout the others down.

Half an hour after Anne and Carly's arrival,
Cliff and Mayor Hilley entered the club together,
and the contrast between Cliff's polished good
looks and the unsophisticated homeliness of
the mayor was striking. Eck Hilley was a good
mayor—he knew the people and their needs—
but he was country-born and country-bred, and
he didn't care who knew it.

While the mayor strode over to the bar to pick
up an ongoing argument with Frank, Cliff placed
his briefcase on the table near Anne. "If you hear
my analysis degenerating into corporate dou-
blespeak, kick me under the table."

She smiled. "Feeling a little desperate?"

Cliff exhaled a heavy sigh and rested his hip
on the table. "We're going to pull this thing off,
Anne, I really believe that, but what am I supposed to tell them? I'm afraid I'll start using
fancy footwork to disguise the fact that I don't
have any hard facts."

"Like the Wizard of Oz?"

"Exactly," he said. "And they don't need fire-
works or smokescreens. They need real answers."

Carly glanced up from the paper she had been
examining. "And do you have answers, real
answers, for them?"

Cliff's lips twisted in a rueful smile. "No,

actually I don't. I have prospects. I have possibilities to offer. I'm afraid that will have to do for now."

While her companions fell into a light debate, Anne studied Cliff, gauging his reaction to Carly. Until that moment Anne hadn't noticed that he held himself differently when the redhead was around. Was Cliff finally getting over the death of his wife?

Moments later Eck Hilley joined them and immediately began the boisterous flattery with which he always greeted Anne. Carly, standing slightly behind the mayor, reacted by poking a finger down her throat and making gagging noises.

Anne glanced away and cleared her throat to keep from laughing. And at that exact moment a man walked into the club, pausing just inside the entrance.

For an instant, for one short moment as she stared at him, Anne felt no reaction at all. Then with dizzying abruptness she felt the blood drain from her face. She couldn't move. She couldn't run. She could only stand and stare, but from somewhere deep inside came the barely formed idea that she had known, that somehow she had expected it would happen in just this way.

Even from a distance the newcomer's rugged features were outstanding. Compelling. He wore faded jeans with a well-worn, brown leather jacket, and his thick, dark-blond hair was mixed with platinum, as though he had spent quite a bit of time in the sun. He looked strong, his body that of a runner rather than a weight lifter, and the way he moved with unrestrained confidence said this was a man you wanted on your side in a fight.

From across the room Anne couldn't make out the color of his eyes, but of course she knew. They were rich, sable brown. Eyes that could warm with incredible heat. Eyes that could freeze the soul. Eyes that were now trained with dark intensity upon her face.

"What's wrong, honey?" Carly asked. "You're shaking all over."

The people around her were still unaware of the stranger who had come recently into their midst, and as they continued to talk, Anne followed their conversation in a removed way, as though the words had to pass through a filter before reaching her.

"I bet you didn't eat dinner," the mayor told her. "I've got a second cousin that does this. He's hyperglaucomic."

"What's that?" Leon asked. "Is it catching?"

"It's kinda like sugar diabetes," Eck explained. "Only different."

"Hypoglycemic, you idiot," Cliff said, moving closer to Anne, his face filled with concern.

"See how white she is," Eck continued. "I tell you the girl needs protein. Frank! You got some milk back there?"

Ignoring the mayor, Cliff followed the direction of Anne's intense concentration. When he spotted the newcomer across the room, his gaze shot back to Anne.

"He's the one—" Cliff broke off abruptly, his

features growing hard as he turned to Leon. "Please tell the gentleman"—he gave a curt nod toward the door—"that the club is closed for repairs. Ask him to leave."

Although Leon frowned, he didn't hesitate. "Sure thing, Mr. Wariner."

By now everyone in the room had noticed the blond man just inside the entrance. They watched Leon approach him, saw the bouncer speak to the man in a low voice, and saw that instead of leaving, the stranger moved farther into the room. When Leon reached out and grasped his arm to stop him, the man simply shook him off and kept walking. Flushing, Leon grabbed the intruder by one shoulder and swung him around abruptly. Then, in what seemed like an effortless movement, the stranger placed one hand on Leon—who was used to intimidating by size alone—and broke the big man's hold.

From behind the bar Frank made an indignant sound of disbelief and jumped over the counter, moving quickly to help his younger brother. "Hold on just a damn minute," he called out. "What in hell do you think you're doing?"

When the bartender reached the two men, he stood close to the stranger, his stance belligerent, his voice raised. "You going to leave, or you want me to call the law?"

Although the newcomer's reply was indistinct, it apparently was not what Frank wanted to hear, because the bartender's face reddened. The scene began to degenerate quickly.

There was Frank, foot and arm flaring as he issued a wild, guttural yell; there was the blond stranger, stepping smoothly out of harm's way with a wry shrug; and there was Leon, his jaw set as he blindly rushed forward to join his older brother. Tables and chairs were overturned, and a tray of glasses crashed to the floor. Eck Hilley began wondering, repeatedly and at the top of his lungs, what in hell was going on, while Carly laughed in delight as she dodged a bowl of pretzels. The wooden bowl missed the redhead, hit the jukebox, and suddenly the chaos had "I Got Friends in Low Places" for background music.

When Anne caught sight of the blond man's face, when she saw the outrageous grin and the gleam of fun in those brown eyes, she felt the same conflicting emotions she had felt on a day so long ago.

Then, seconds later, a smear of blood on the newcomer's lip brought Anne abruptly out of her trance. "Cliff," she said, her voice low and urgent, "this isn't necessary. Make them stop."

Frank, who now sat on the floor propped against the bar, was nursing his jaw, but Leon, his head lowered, his teeth clenched, was still trying to land punches.

"Leon!" Cliff called out. "That's enough."

When Leon moved away reluctantly, the stranger turned and looked at Cliff, his gaze dropping to take in the older man's dark business suit. "You people take your dress code real serious, don't you?" he said. "Next time I'll make sure I'm wearing a tie."

Although no one responded, everyone in the room was watching him closely. He in turn was watching Anne. He didn't take his eyes from her as he moved across the room, not even when he reached up to wipe the blood from his mouth with the back of his hand.

Moments later, when he stood directly in front of her, his lips eased into a slow smile.

"Hello, Annie," he said softly. "Long time no see."

Three

Anne stood perfectly still—she barely breathed—
as she stared at him with unblinking concentration. *Max*. He was here, not a foot away from
her.

Anne had dreamed this reunion a thousand
times. And now, as in her dreams, her emotions
were so confused that she didn't know how to
deal with them. There was sorrow and regret
and longing, mixed together in a sad little pot-
pourri. But overriding those useless emotions
were two others. Two powerful emotions that
fought for supremacy: overwhelming joy . . .
and fear.

"Anne?"

Distracted by the sharply spoken query, Anne
pulled her gaze away from his face and found
Cliff close at her side, his features strained with
worry.

"Cliff," she said slowly, then gave her head a little shake. "I'm sorry, this is—Could someone unplug the jukebox? Everyone, this is Max Decatur. Max . . . my boss, Cliff Wariner. And my good friend, Carly Angelo."

Max smiled and nodded at the two people who were watching him with varying degrees of curiosity.

"Eck Hilley," she continued, "the mayor of Emily . . ."

"Your Honor."

". . . and I think you've already met Leon and Frank Carter."

"Leon . . . Frank," Max said with a friendly wave in the direction of the bar.

Leon mumbled, "Pleased to meetcha" through the towel he held pressed to his nose, but his brother didn't look up as he limped toward the jukebox.

When Frank jerked the jukebox cord from the outlet, the room was suddenly engulfed in silence. Max stood looking at Anne, while everyone else looked at Max.

Pushing a curl off her forehead, Anne cleared her throat. "We could—" She broke off and glanced at Cliff. "Has everything been cleared out of the Cedar Room?" When he gave a short nod, she turned back to Max. "We could go into one of the private dining rooms if you want to"—she swallowed heavily—"talk."

"Sure, that's fine," he said, and followed her out of the main room.

Near the end of the dimly lighted hall Anne opened a door, switched on the overhead light, and stepped into a small room, flinching slightly when she heard the door close. *This is it,* she told herself. She had always known this day would come. She was prepared for it. She could handle it. Sweaty palms, a dry mouth, and a hyperactive heartbeat were no big deal. *I will survive . . . whether I want to or not.* Drawing in a deep, slow breath, she turned to face him.

He stood leaning against the closed door, staring at her with such concentrated interest that it brought the blood rushing back to her face.

She waited. And as she waited, she took note of the changes in him. Some were obvious, some more subtle. Time had etched a network of fine lines around his eyes; the vulnerable look of first youth was gone. As a result his features were stronger and even more striking.

Pushing away from the door, he took a step toward her. "Hello, Annie," he said again in his husky voice.

Taking an involuntary step backward, she opened her mouth to speak, then shook her head helplessly. There were so many things she wanted to say, so many things she *needed* to say. She had played the scene over and over in her mind, composing in detail what she would say to him and how he would react. But now, when she finally had the chance, the words wouldn't come together. All she could do was watch in mute fascination as he took another step toward her.

"Hello, Annie."

She frowned, eyes narrowed as she drew back

her head. This wasn't how it was supposed to happen. Never—in none of her imaginary confrontations—did she feel annoyed by the friend-lover who had long haunted her waking and sleeping dreams.

"Would you stop saying 'Hello, Annie' like some—"

She broke off abruptly as she backed into a table, then an instant later her breath left her in a soft whoosh as he grabbed her and, wrapping his arms around her, pulled her close against his hard body.

"I can't believe it," he said, hugging her tightly. "Annie. Little Annie with the smoky eyes. This is really wild. Imagine running into you like this. I only got into town tonight. I was just driving around, checking out the town, then—" He laughed. "Talk about serendipity. I haven't seen or heard from you in over eleven years, and suddenly there you are. It was—"

"Max . . . *Max*!"

Easing out of his arms, she murmured, "What's wrong with this scene?" under her breath, then raised her eyes to his. "Why aren't you trying to strangle me? Why aren't you screaming at me, calling me names?"

He laughed, giving her a glimpse of the sexy, solitary dimple. "Still the same. You've always met things head-on, no matter how scared you were."

"With one notable exception," she said, the reminder both rueful and wary.

"Is that what's worrying you? That all happened a long time ago, and life is too short to go around holding grudges." He hopped up on the table, casually swinging his legs. "We grew up together. You, Ellie, and I—we were like family. We've got a history, squirt. Nothing could change that."

"But—" she began, but when he smiled down at her, every thought, every doubt vanished in a flood tide of warmth. How could she resist that smile? She had been deprived of his smile for eleven years, and she didn't care what might happen tomorrow or even an hour from now. She only wanted to stand near the warmth for a while. *Please God, just for a little while.*

"This is wild," he said. "I saw Ellie just a few months ago, and we were both wondering what happened to you." He laughed, the infectious, irresistible laugh she remembered so well. "Remember the time I was Superman and Ellie was Cat Woman and she tied you up and left you in that toolshed? Then she forgot where she put you, and it took us all afternoon to find you again. I was going crazy, imagining you scared out of your mind, but when we finally found you, you were sitting there singing. All tied up like a freakin' Christmas turkey, and you were *singing.* That blew me away."

Anne laughed. "I haven't thought about that in years." The incident hadn't stuck in her mind because although she had been afraid, she had never doubted that Max would find her. He always found her.

"You were furious," she said, "yelling and kicking the wall. For a minute I was afraid you were going to give Ellie a black eye."

"I would have if she hadn't started crying. That's when I realized she'd been as scared as I was. You were so little. So damned fragile. God, it's good to see you again, squirt. You know, I thought I saw you last week in San Antonio."

Anne caught her breath. "I was in San Antonio. Just three days ago. You—you were there?"

"You mean it really was you?" Max said, watching her face. "That's weird. Going all that time without running into each other, then twice in one week."

Play it light, he told himself. *Remember what's at stake.* Seeing her up close had thrown him for a moment. He had told himself a million times that he was building her up in his imagination, making her more than she really was. But none of his fantasies, none of his vivid daydreams, had done her justice. None had come close to reality.

And finding that the emotions he had felt on an ordinary San Antonio street were magnified a hundredfold with propinquity was a bitter pill to swallow. He had to keep reminding himself that he was in control this time. This time there would be no surprises.

"It must have been fate," he said, smiling at her. "It was simply time for the three of us to get together again. Ellie will have a fit when I tell her I found you. You were always more of a sister to her than those two witches she shares a bloodline with. She's really missed you, Annie."

Without thinking, he reached out and pulled her toward him, fitting her body close between his thighs. Instantly he realized his mistake.

His hands on her hips began to shake, and perspiration beaded his upper lip.

Glancing quickly away from her, he moved her to the side and slid off the table. "Listen, I know you have stuff going on," he said as he walked toward the door. "I didn't know if that out there"—he nodded toward the main room—"was a stag party or a secret meeting, but—"

"Oh, Max," she broke in, her voice as distracted as her gray eyes, "I'm sorry about Leon and Frank. They're all good people, really they are. Cliff just got the wrong idea about—I mean, he didn't understand what our relationship was."

"Didn't he?"

Max's lips twitched in a slight smile. Cliff wasn't the only one who didn't understand. Annie didn't understand either. But she would.

Anne had been watching him closely, and she felt a little of her tension drain away when he suddenly laughed and shook his head. "I didn't mind the fight, but all those weighty silences made me feel like I was breaking in on a scene from Pinter. Anyway, I'll get out of your way for now. We can catch up later," he said as he turned and opened the door. "I'm staying over at—"

"Hufstedtler's," she finished for him. "Unit Ten?"

Anne smiled when his eyes widened in surprise. "No, I haven't developed psychic abilities," she told him. "The tourist court is the only place in town. And Joe Mack always puts people he doesn't recognize in Ten."

"Does Unit Ten have a peephole?" he asked warily. "And does Joe Mack live with his bony little mama?"

"No, but the carpet is only four years old, and if Joe Mack doesn't know you, you might be someone worth impressing."

"I see. Has his prudence ever paid off?" he asked as he moved through the doorway.

"Not until now," she murmured, then added, "Wait. Max . . . you didn't tell me why you're here. In Emily, I mean."

"I'm looking for faces."

And then, as abruptly as he had appeared, Max was gone.

"You know what kind of men you meet in motel bars? Software salesmen," Carly said as she negotiated the curves on the narrow road to Anne's house. "But not her, not Diane Harper. She meets a gorgeous six-foot hunk who got hit on the head with a bronze statue so he doesn't remember that he's the head of an international shipping company instead of a waiter who needs a haircut and— Why do I keep watching the stupid show when I know good and well . . ."

Although Anne heard the words, they didn't penetrate. The same thing had happened at the council meeting. She assumed Cliff's presentation had gone well, but she couldn't swear to it. Then as now, her mind had been somewhere else.

". . . and at first I thought I must have misunderstood her," Carly was saying. "But she said it at least three times in a single conversation. Talk about careless casting. I could have played the part with one hand tied behind my back. This woman is supposed to be a doctor, for Pete's sake. You'd think a brain surgeon would know how to pronounce *sandwich*. A brain surgeon who's actually the Princess Ravela von Leinsdorf in disguise. And she asks for a ham-and-cheese *samich*?"

Several seconds passed before Anne realized Carly had stopped talking. "I'm sorry," she apologized. "My mind was wandering. You were talking about . . ."

"Go ahead, tell me what I was talking about," the redhead urged, giving a skeptical laugh as the Dodge coughed and sputtered to a halt beside Anne's house. "You didn't hear a word I said. Never mind. Are you going to invite me in for coffee?"

Inside the house Anne led the way to the kitchen as Carly muttered, "I've been patient. You have to admit I've been patient, but enough is enough. I'm warning you right now, Anne, I'm gonna ask. Anne . . . *Anne*, talk to me!"

"Talk?" Anne murmured as she pushed open the door to the kitchen. "How can I talk when I can't think?" Swinging abruptly around, she collided with Carly, and grasping the redhead's shoulders, she gave her a vigorous shake. "Images . . . sounds . . . wild ideas, all swirling around in my brain, ricocheting off each other with little twanging noises."

Carly studied her face. "I've never seen you like this. You're hyper. Electrified. You're—"

"Alive?" Anne offered with a soft, wry laugh. "Anne was in a lonely place, Carly, with wind whistling down the corridors, but I'm stepping out of the shadows now. And it's warm here. It's bright and—"

"It's damned weird here," the redhead interrupted, watching her warily.

Turning away from the questions in Carly's eyes, Anne began to make coffee. When she felt calmer, she glanced at the other woman. "I'm seeing so much. I mean, now that I'm awake, I can see how— You're supposed to be my best friend. Why didn't you tell me I had turned into a weenie? I lost my backbone. For eleven years I've been acting like a kicked dog, slinking around in the shadows, afraid to make any kind of definitive move in case someone noticed and kicked me again."

"Who kicked you the first time?"

Anne shrugged. "Life . . . fate . . . circumstance . . . Murphy's Law. That doesn't matter. What matters is that I let it kill all the life in me. I used to laugh, Carly," she said softly. "And I used to shout. I used to have emphatic emotions." She shook her head. "Why did I let all that die?"

"Why are you asking me?" Carly asked, her voice sharp with frustration. "More important, *what* are you asking me? So far I've understood maybe one word in ten. Just be quiet and let me think a minute."

Both women stood next to the counter, silently watching the glass pot fill with coffee. When it was half full, Carly moved to lean her hip against the counter. "Okay . . . okay, so you're stepping back into the light and all that stuff. And we'll take it as said that I'm pleased as punch that you're no longer a wuss. The thing is, your transmutation leads me to one vital question: Who the hell is Max?"

"Who is Max? Who is *Max*?" Grabbing the redhead's hand, Anne hauled her out of the kitchen and into the hall.

"I'll show you who the hell Max is," she said as she moved into her small office and flipped on the overhead light. Waving a hand at the bookshelves that lined one wall, she said, "That's Max."

"A librarian?" Carly frowned her confusion. "A carpenter? Could you be a little more specific?"

Anne stepped forward. "He's on this shelf . . . from here to here."

Joining her, Carly picked up one of the books. Upon opening it, she whistled through her teeth. "Grizzly stuff," she murmured. "I don't have the courage to look at pictures of war. Is this Afghanistan? Is he a war correspondent?"

Although Anne gave no reply, Carly didn't notice. The redhead was being seduced by the images depicted in the slim volume. After a slow examination of several pages, she said, "The man responsible for this is no reporter. He's an artist. But what kind of art uses human suffering?"

Again Anne held her silence. She wanted Carly to reach her own conclusions about Max's work, and for several minutes the slow turning of pages was the only sound in the office.

"I was wrong," Carly said finally. "You have to look at the whole thing. This juxtaposition of raw brutality against reawakening beauty tells a story. It's about hope, isn't it?" She met Anne's eyes. "It's gripping stuff. Definitely not for casual perusal, because it gets your soul stirred up, whether you want it or not."

Reaching out, Anne turned the book over. Carly stared at the back-cover photo of Max for a moment, then glanced back at the shelf where there were two other books and dozens of magazines. "This is all his work?"

"Most of it," Anne confirmed. She pulled out a magazine and smiled as it fell open to the page she wanted. "This was taken by someone else."

It was a Harley-Davidson ad, and on the far right, barely in the picture, was a beautiful, dark-haired woman. Her expression was obviously sensual, but in her dark eyes was a devilish gleam, a look of mischief, as though she were about to double over laughing. A younger Max was in the center, straddling the metal monster with his feet planted firmly on asphalt. He was dressed in black leather, but it was the man rather than the clothes that drew the eye. As he stared straight into the camera, his features were aloof, almost sullen. The barely repressed hostility didn't in any way repel. It pulled the onlooker in against her will, urging her to get closer to the danger, closer to the untamed, undisguised sexuality.

Carly fanned her face vigorously with one

hand. "Is it getting hot in here? Sweet Caesar, looking at him feels like foreplay." She paused. "This woman . . . I've seen her before, Elise Something Something. She was in all those heavy-on-symbolism perfume commercials a few years back."

"Elise Adler Bright," Anne confirmed. "That shelf, the one below Max's, belongs to Ellie."

"Ellie?"

Anne moved away from the bookshelves. "The three of us grew up together. And we had only each other. Ellie's father lived in a world of his own. Max's aunt—his legal guardian—couldn't stand the sight of him. My mother saw me mostly as an inconvenience. There was no affection between us. I can't remember her ever hugging me. By rights I probably should have turned into a sociopath. But I didn't because I had friends. Ellie, Max, and Annie—we were a unit. The fingers of a tightly clenched fist." She let out a slow breath. "Now Ellie is rich and famous, just as she always said she would be. And Max has traveled all over the world as one of the country's top photographers, as he said he would."

"And Annie? What did she say she would be?"

"Annie said she would be Max's wife."

Carly raised one brow in surprised interest. "That was your only ambition?"

Anne laughed. "That surprises you, doesn't it? You, my militant friend, would have set a higher goal for me, something that emphasized the strength and ingenuity of womankind." She shook her head slowly. "For me it was not only my goal, it was my reason for existing. God created me specifically for the purpose of loving Max. And that's all there was to it."

Carly stared at her hands for a moment, then looked up and met her friend's gaze. "I'm sorry. I'm sorry it didn't work out for you. If you loved him that much . . . if he still affects you as much as he obviously does— Back at the Longhorn, you looked like a piano had fallen on you. If this is the reason that haunted, hunted look comes over you, then I'm sorry you didn't get to marry your Max."

Anne turned away from the compassion in Carly's eyes and walked to the window, staring out into the darkness. "But I did," she said softly. "I did marry my Max."

Four

Carly simply stared. At one point she started to say something, but she stopped and, with her mouth still open, dropped abruptly to the leather davenport.

"You married him?" the redhead said finally. "You were married to *him*?"

"Close your mouth."

Obeying, Carly closed her mouth, but not for long. "I had no idea you were this interesting," she said, surveying Anne from top to bottom.

"Excuse me?"

"You know what I mean." The redhead ran a hand through her unruly hair. "You've been going around like a plainclothes nun, and all the time you had *him* in your background. When did . . . I mean, how long has it been since you've seen him?"

"Eleven years," Anne said, her voice as distracted as her thoughts. The euphoria that had held her for hours was beginning to fade, and confusion was taking its place. "He should have been—He should hate me, Carly. I expected that. I was prepared for that. I always thought that when we met again—I never doubted that we would meet again, but I thought it would be different. In my mind's eye I could see and feel his anger. Contempt . . . even hatred. But he acted as though nothing had happened between us, as though we were old friends meeting again after years of being apart."

Carly had been staring at the wall, but now she turned her head around to look at Anne. "Why do I get the feeling that you're not pleased about that?"

"I'm pleased," she said, but her voice was unconvincing even to her own ears. "But, well, maybe I thought, when he had punished me, when I *paid* for what I did—Don't look at me like that. I haven't suddenly turned masochist. I'm not going to fall to my knees and say 'Please, master, hurt me.' There's a principle involved. Eleven years ago I didn't give him a chance to react. It was a hit-and-run kind of thing. And even though he doesn't seem to want to hit back, the injustice is still there."

When the redhead shot a skeptical look in her direction, Anne sighed. "No, you're right. I'm not that much of a saint. The punishment wasn't entirely for justice. It was for me too. I thought if he retaliated in some way, it would be over. I thought that it would finally be over."

Carly studied her for a moment. "I don't know

what you did to him," she said slowly, "but if you think you haven't paid for it, you're crazy."

Anne shook her head. "It's not enough. What I've done to myself, living in a state of hibernation, could bring him no satisfaction. Compensation should be made to him. Equity demands that I make payment directly to *him*."

"So what you're saying is he cheated you. He cheated you out of peace of mind. If he had hit you and called you a low-down bitch, you could have finally gotten on with your life. But because he's ignoring this mysterious dastardly deed, you're still stuck with guilt." Carly's smile wasn't pleasant. "I'd say that was a pretty slick move on his part."

Agitated, Anne stood up. "No. He isn't doing this intentionally. Max isn't like that. He simply did what I haven't managed to do. He put the past in the past. He was genuinely glad to see me."

Pressing both hands to her hot cheeks, she closed her eyes. "I still can't take it in, Carly. Just this afternoon, only hours ago, I was sitting out on the terrace doing my Omar Khayyám number, and—"

"Hold on, you've lost me again," Carly said. "Now we're talking about a loaf of bread and a jug of wine?"

"No, all those other rubáiyáts. You know, descending into dust, 'sans wine, sans song, sans singer . . . sans end.' That stuff. I was feeling my nights and days slipping away. Regretting that I have no children, regretting the past. 'Unborn tomorrow and dead yesterday.'"

"Stop, you're depressing me . . . and I have a kid. I suppose you got around to that old Flying Fickle Finger of Fate as well?"

"That too," Anne said with a breathless laugh. "I was pretty much wallowing in it."

Carly studied her face. "This afternoon, when Petey and I were here, that wasn't about going to the prom with a short cousin. That was about Max, wasn't it?"

With an almost imperceptible nod, Anne moved to sit on the corner of her desk. "'Turn down an empty glass,'" she quoted softly. "That's what I've been doing. For most of my adult life I've been turning down an empty glass for Max."

Throwing back her head, Anne drew in a deep breath. "He's back, Carly. Max is back in my life. It doesn't matter that his being here is a fluke, or that it's not permanent. It doesn't even matter that he—" She cleared her throat. "That he sees me only as childhood friend."

Anne winced as a sharp little pain stabbed her temples. A childhood friend? *You're a whore just like your mother!*

When the room grew suddenly airless, making it difficult for her to catch her breath, Anne gave her head a sharp shake, rejecting the old familiar fear, pushing it away with an almost physical effort.

"None of that matters," she said with growing confidence. "It only matters that he's back in my life, and sooner or later I'll hear him say that he's forgiven me."

Carly moved to the desk, leaning her hip against it as she studied Anne's face. "Are you sure you want to stir things up? You said he's put it all behind him. Can't you take the forgiveness part as a done deal?"

Raising her head, Anne met her friend's eyes. "I need the words, Carly. I need to see his face when he says the words."

"And if he doesn't want to say them?"

Anne frowned. "I don't know. I guess I'll have to force the issue. He'll either say he forgives me, or he'll admit that deep down he's still angry. I can handle either one."

Pushing away from the desk, Carly said, "Hey, I'm with you. For good or for bad. That's the nice part of having a best friend who's been around the block. We don't run for cover when the shooting starts." She scratched her chin and raised one brow. "You okay now? If you want, I can stay and we can talk . . . or even not talk. We could watch television . . . listen to music . . . try some new hairstyles . . . get drunk?"

Anne laughed. "I'm fine. Really. Go home to Petey."

As soon as she had closed the door behind Carly, Anne walked back to her study and began returning the books and magazines to the shelves. But after a moment her movements stilled and her gaze was drawn irresistibly toward her desk.

In the lower right-hand drawer was a piece of Maximilian Decatur memorabilia that she had neglected to mention to Carly. Anne had put it in the desk so she wouldn't see it, so she wouldn't come across it by accident when she was looking at his work.

Walking to the desk, she reached down, opened the bottom drawer, and pulled out a magazine. It was a high-gloss, we're-so-glad-we're-not-ordinary-like-you kind of publication, and there on the cover was Max, along with the words WILL THE REAL MAXIMILIAN DECATUR PLEASE STAND UP?

When she sat down and placed the magazine on her lap, it automatically fell open to the article. The first page was text, a lightweight accounting of an artistic genius that—in Anne's opinion—in no way resembled the real Max. The facing page was a montage of small black-and-white photos. One showed him looking unfamiliar but elegant in a tuxedo as he arrived at a showing of his work in Chicago. In another he was hunkered down on his heels as he participated in a Native American religious ceremony. Her favorite showed Max with his head thrown back as he shared laughter with a chubby, big-eyed Tibetan child.

These were pictures Anne could handle. It was the two full-page photographs on the following pages that she had trouble dealing with.

Closing the magazine, she stared at the wall with unseeing eyes. The photographs, each and every one of them, had been taken by Genna Reynolds. In the sixties Genna's husband, Mc-Neal Reynolds, had become one of the world's most respected photographers. He was also the man under whom Max had served his apprenticeship. Eleven years ago Anne had met McNeal Reynolds. And Genna.

It was at a party that was out of Annie Seaton Decatur's league. Way, way out. Anne, with her Alice in Wonderland hair and her homecoming dance dress, had known she was in over her head even before Max had introduced her to his mentor's wife. Genna Reynolds was thirteen years older than Anne, and there had been a sensuality about her that was so blatant, so provocative, that it had made Anne uneasy. And as young as she had been, as unworldly as she had been, Anne had known immediately and without a doubt that Genna wanted Max.

"Oh boy, did she want him," Anne whispered.

She let the magazine fall open again to the article, and slowly she turned the page.

Both full-page photographs were intensely personal; both felt like an intrusion of Max's privacy. The article's author had been honest enough to admit they had been taken without the subject's knowledge or consent, adding that Max was an inordinately private person who wanted his work on view rather than his person. Apparently the journalist had understated the case. Genna had sold the photographs years after they were taken, and soon after the magazine hit the stands, Max had disappeared into a Japanese jungle.

Steeling herself, Anne lowered her gaze again to the magazine. The first photograph showed a solitary figure in profile—Max raising his eyes to a vast and dramatic African sky. The loneliness and pain etched into his unforgettable features brought a lump to her throat and made the portrait difficult to look at.

On the opposite page Max again stood alone. But this photograph was full front. He stood close to some sort of watering trough and was in the process of cooling off with handfuls of water. His chest was bare, and his jeans were unfastened, hanging low, barely covering his lower abdomen. A myriad of diamond droplets sparkled in the sun as they joined the tanned flesh of his chest and stomach. This view of Max made the observer uneasy as well, but in a different, far more physical way.

Rising abruptly to her feet, Anne left the study and didn't stop until she had reached the terrace. Inhaling the scent of the river, she fell into silent argument. She wasn't going to fool herself into believing they could start over again; on a night eleven years ago she had made sure that would never happen. But even if she could never make him understand the reasons behind her actions, even if she deserved no absolution, forgiveness would cost him nothing. He no longer loved her, and apparently the pain she had caused was only a distant memory. Max had always been generous. Sooner or later he would say the words.

Wrapping her arms tightly around her waist, she tried to contain the feverish excitement, tried to hold still the deep pleasure. Max was here, and it was going to be all right again. She could never be his special, forever love, she told herself as she turned toward the house. But she could be his friend. She could be his family again.

• • •

The next day Anne saw Max three times from a distance, and each time he waved and called, "Yo, Annie!" with laughter in his voice. At first she felt warmed, but gradually she realized this new, slightly distant relationship was going to take some getting used to.

When Anne was growing up, she had Max. Definitely, without question. Then for the next decade she had been without him. Definitely, without question. Now he was here, but he wasn't hers. And that was what was causing her disorientation. In the past she had had all of him, or she had had nothing. She didn't know how to have Max slightly in her life.

That night after dinner Anne waited for him to call, but except for a call from Petey to tell her he had found his little shovel, the phone didn't ring.

He's busy, she told herself as she stood beside the telephone, willing it to ring. He had things to take care of, faces to scope out.

But on the other hand, maybe he was waiting for her to call. This was Anne's territory. Maybe she should call him and arrange to take him around town and introduce him to the people of Emily.

She had the phone in her hand and had dialed the first three numbers of Hufstedtler's when she dropped the receiver back into place and shoved her hands into the pockets of her robe. Max had never been shy. It he wanted her help, he would ask for it.

With a restless sigh she turned away from the silent telephone and went to bed, but only after hours of restless tossing and turning did she finally fall asleep.

The darkness surrounding Anne was complete. No spark or beam of light, no tiny scrap of color, was allowed to break through. The shadows were so strong, so thick, they burned her nostrils and clogged her throat.

From the moment the darkness overtook her, Anne truly believed that it was as powerful as the fear, but then came real understanding: The darkness was the fear. It contained the fear and was contained by it.

Nothing could have been more appalling, nothing more unendurable, than the all-encompassing blackness. And so it seemed . . . until the emptiness reached her.

The void came first from a distance, a weak but constant force that slid across her flesh with lonely fingers. Then without warning it began to expand, growing colder and stronger with each moment that passed. Advancing and retreating, swelling and spreading, the barren maelstrom increased to awesome proportions in its attempt to suck the life from every hidden corner of the darkness.

As panic held her motionless, the outcome seemed inevitable. She was going to suffocate. Alone in the unrelenting darkness, she was going to be crushed alive by the emptiness.

Then across the gulf of darkness, a voice

reached out to her. "Hush, now, Annie. It's going to be all right."

It was a miracle, these words that came to her from beyond the crushing desolation, resonating with strength and security, reaching out to pull her away from the fear.

"You don't have to stay there, Annie," the voice assured her. "Come to me, where it's safe and warm and bright. Follow me, Annie. There's life here. You can have it too. Just follow me."

"I can't!" she screamed into the darkness. "Where are you? I can't find you! I can't—"

When Anne came fully awake, she was sitting up in bed, her face and throat bathed with perspiration. As her breathing gradually returned to normal, she focused on the moonlight that fell in polished pewter streams through the window.

Although it was a familiar dream, she had never grown used to it. It still disturbed her to find that in reality, there was no impenetrable darkness, no unquenchable void, and that there was no strong, confident voice that wanted to keep her safe.

Pushing her tangled hair from her face, she climbed out of bed. Fifteen minutes later she had pulled her hair back in a loose French braid and was dressed in white jeans and a cranberry cotton-knit sweater. She left the house to walk toward the river. Her old friend.

There was chill in the air and a coating of dew

on the grass as Anne stood on the riverbank to watch the last of the moonlight being absorbed by the awakening sun. Across the river brilliant color began to fill every crack and crevice of the smudged-charcoal line of trees.

The miracle held her still, and she stood waiting, waiting for the wonder to fill the trees, then spill over to the river, until finally it would reach her.

Then several feet away, on her side of the river, one of the shadows moved toward her, changing, becoming a tall man in khaki slacks, tan shirt, and a worn leather jacket.

"Max," she said, the word a slightly squeaky whisper. "You scared me."

"Guilty conscience?" Before she could respond, he said, "You looked like you were going into a trance. I don't know what comes next in the ceremony, but discretion demanded I interrupt you now . . . before you got naked or anything."

Laughing, she said, "I don't carry my nature worship quite that far." She glanced around. "I didn't hear a car. How did you get here?"

He nodded toward a point down river. "I rented a cabin half a mile or so that way."

"A cabin? Wait a minute, don't tell me you let Billy Loomis sucker you into renting that rat hole of his?"

Grinning, he shook his head. "It's not that bad. I wanted to be close to the river, so it was either the Loomis cabin or a sleeping bag."

"On your head be it," she said doubtfully. "You looked as if you were having a good time checking out the natives yesterday. How do you like Emily so far?"

"It takes some getting used to." He ran a hand across his unshaven jaw. "They've built a kind of invisible wall around the place, and what's happening in the rest of the world doesn't quite reach here. Oh, they hear about it, but a disaster on Wall Street doesn't affect them as much as seeing Fred's pickup parked in front of Rita's house on Friday night does. I guess it's the same with all small towns. Anyway it's perfect for what I had in mind."

"Which is?" she asked, watching him closely.

"When the six-o'clock news does a story on the economy, they show a couple of out-of-work executives or a few construction workers. It's always city dwellers. I wanted to show what happens to small-town people when a recession hits. Losing the steel mill has devastated this place. And the loss is multiplied because it's not only happening to you, it's happening to your next-door neighbor, your brother-in-law, and the guy you bowl with on Tuesday nights." He paused and reached up to rub the back of his neck. "It's the most close-knit community I've ever come across. They all know I'm a friend of yours, by the way. And they're not real subtle about the way they feel about you." He smiled. "The place is just oozing with down-home, just-plain-folks loyalty."

It was an innocent remark, but something in his tone disturbed her. "Max, you're not . . . you wouldn't—" She broke off and tried to gather her thoughts. "You've been to a lot of places, seen a lot of things. You've led a sophisticated life and mixed with sophisticated people. Emily is not—No, that's not what I wanted to say." She shook her head and began again. "You said you were looking for faces, but these people, they're more than just faces. They're hearts and souls. These people, Max, they'll welcome you. They'll ask you into their homes. They won't even mind talking about having no money. They'll show you the empty cupboards and the piles of unpaid bills. They won't think about what you're going to do with your pictures. They won't know that their . . . their honest naïveté might be interpreted as backwardness by the rest of the world. They'll think it's strange that outsiders could possibly be interested in them, but they'll also think it's exciting. They'll buy the book or magazine and show it to their relatives in the city." She paused. "They won't know what people are thinking of them, but I will, Max. I'll know, and I'll be angry for them."

Long, tense moments passed before he turned to face her. "You think I'd do that?" His lips quirked in a strange smile, as though his amusement had turned inward, toward something only he could see. "You think I'll show them in that kind of light?"

She couldn't answer. After shrugging in a helpless movement, she simply stared at him in silence.

Scratching the top of his head, he glanced around. "Well, I guess I'd better be running along. See you around, Annie," he added as he turned and walked away.

She watched him for a moment with something almost like fear welling up in her throat. She took a step after him. "Wait," she said softly, then she called out louder, "Max . . . *wait for me!*"

And then she was running after him, just as she had done so many times when she was a little girl. She had to catch up with him. She had to reach him before he disappeared again.

"Max." She was breathless when she caught at his arm, trying to stop him. Pausing, he looked down at her, allowing her to examine his features. Even now there was no anger in his features, no sadness. He simply looked interested.

"I'm sorry. I was wrong," she said, fighting to catch her breath. "You have to understand—" She clasped his right hand between both of hers and whispered, "Please accept my most sincere and humble apology, O great and magnificent Maximilian . . . please, Max."

When he threw back his head and laughed, Anne knew it was going to be all right. He wasn't going to leave.

"You're not still worried about me taking advantage of your people?" he asked.

She shook her head vehemently. "No, that was stupid. It was just something I thought I heard, something I thought I saw in your face." She felt his fingers move under hers. "It doesn't matter now. You wouldn't hurt them."

"No, I wouldn't hurt them." Freeing his hand, he shoved it inside his jacket pocket and stood studying the sunrise. "When I was in Afghanistan, I met a guy, a fellow photographer. Rick taught me a lot. He was older, and tougher, I guess. He covered Vietnam and came through it unscathed, physically and emotionally." He shook his head in disbelief. "It didn't touch him. Rick was always looking for that Pulitzer prize–winning shot. He wasn't interested in the people. I don't think he even admitted to himself that they *were* people. All he cared about was the perfect picture. He wanted to capture agony, but not just your average, everyday kind of agony. He wanted the spectacular stuff. He wanted to catch the body the moment the land mine exploded under it. He wanted to capture the helicopter at the exact second it exploded in the air."

Max paused and drew in a slow breath. "After spending one night in a bar with Rick Ord, I took a good look at my soul. That wasn't fun. Because when I looked deep enough, I found a bloody mess. But at least it still existed. It was still there, and it was still working. I promised myself right then that I would never get to the point of placing my work above my humanity. I promised myself that if I ever—even once—felt Rick's detachment creeping up on me, I would shoot only stills. Scenery suitable for calendars, travel folders, and books that decorate coffee tables."

Anne had been staring at her shoes, but now she slowly raised her head. "I apologize again," she said in a rough whisper. "I knew that about you. I've seen you work, and I *knew* that. I just got sidetracked for a minute. I really am sorry. I was so excited about seeing you this morning, then I had to go and spoil it. I want—"

"What do you want, Annie?" he asked softly.

Moistening her lips in a nervous gesture, she realized that the inward-turned amusement was back in his voice. "I hope I want the same thing you want. I want to . . . reclaim a relationship that means—has always meant—a lot to me. You were the single most important person in my life," she said with quiet intensity. "I . . . I just want to know that you—"

Slinging one arm around her, he gave her a quick hug. "If you're trying to say you missed me, the feeling is mutual, squirt." He raised a questioning brow. "So if I promise not to make fun of the good citizens of Emily, will you show me around town, introduce me to your friends? Don't take this wrong, but I have a feeling that if I tell them I want to take pictures, they'll get dressed up in their Sunday best and show me into the parlor."

She laughed. "That's exactly what they'd do," she said in affectionate amusement.

When he said, "I gather they're having a pretty rough time right now," she spent the following minutes explaining to him about the project she and Cliff were working on, telling him about the unified support of the people in Emily.

"They're amazing," she said finally. "Pride and strength are not qualities they have to think about or look for. They're just there. Like Mr. Hayes. Oh, Max, you'll love Mr. Hayes. His face looks like one of those dried-apple dolls. And Lacey Cobb. I swear she looks like old Russian royalty. She still lives on the farm she and her husband bought in the twenties, and she does all her own cooking and cleaning. She's wonderful. You've got to meet her. Wait, I know."

They had been walking side by side, but now she swung around to face him, excitement growing as she thought of all the friends she wanted to share with him. "I know what we can do, Max. We can—"

The words died away abruptly as she realized that Max wasn't listening. With a blank look in his eyes, he was staring down at her, staring at the hand that lay on his arm, staring at the way her body was almost but not quite touching his.

She wasn't sure who moved, but suddenly they were touching. Her breasts were pressed against his chest and one of his hands rested on her hip. Awareness raced through her like an electric shock, tightening her nipples, rippling through her groin. Losing rational thought, she stood on her tiptoes, straining to fit her body to his, her lips tingling in anticipation of the kiss that surely would come next.

But it didn't. When Max muttered, "Sweet merciful heaven" under his breath, his fingers digging painfully into the flesh of her buttocks, Anne was brought back to earth with painful swiftness.

Stepping quickly away from him, she whispered, "Lord, Max, I'm sorry." Unable to meet his eyes, she turned her back on him, clenching her hands at her sides. "That was so *stupid*," she said, her voice stiff with embarrassment. "Stupid, stupid, *stupid*! I can't believe I did that.

Why do I keep making a fool of myself with you?"

She flinched when she felt his hand on her shoulder. He turned her around to face him, and although she thought he had lost color under his tan, he was smiling at her. "Hey, lighten up. It was no big deal. It's kind of like LSD. Years later you're going along, minding your own business, and suddenly you're in the middle of a wild trip. Flashback time."

Flashback time. With a few words the love they had once shared was reduced to a malfunction of the brain. It just didn't feel right. While she was glad that he had managed to ease her away from embarrassment, part of her resented the way he diminished what they had been to each other in the past. Their relationship might not have been perfect, but it had been powerful. It had been *real*.

"It felt like a big deal from my side," she said slowly. Then, drawing her head back, she added, "What do you know about LSD trips anyway?"

"My knowledge is purely academic, I assure you," he said, grinning.

"It had better be. Because you wouldn't even let me take a drag off a cigarette when I was a kid." Glancing at her watch, she grimaced. "Oh, my gosh, I've got to pack," she exclaimed as she suddenly recalled the trip to Houston. "Cliff's going to murder me. I can't believe I forgot."

As she talked, she was already walking toward the house, but then she paused, realizing that Max was no longer beside her.

Turning around to walk backward, she called,

"We'll only be gone a couple of days. You won't— I'll see you when I get back, won't I?"

After only a brief hesitation he smiled. "I'm not going anywhere."

Five

Max stood on the corner, looking around Emily. Annie's town wasn't much to look at. In fact he could see most of it from where he was. There wasn't even a traffic light. A four-way stop was as urban as it got in Emily.

To the northwest, surrounded by live oaks and cedars, was the courthouse, which looked as though it had been built around the time Orville and Wilbur were doing their thing in Kitty Hawk. To the northeast was a row of shops with names like the Mercantile and House of Fudge. Across the street from Max was Katie's Kountry Krafts, and behind him was a bank with pink geraniums and two drive-through windows.

Max had been walking around for approximately fifteen minutes, and so far an even dozen people had waved to him. A few of them he had met; most he didn't know from Adam. That took some getting used to. It was friendly, but it also gave him the feeling that he was constantly being watched. In Dallas or Houston he could have hung around on the corner for a couple of weeks without attracting any attention. Apparently anonymity didn't exist in Emily.

Annie had been gone for a little over twenty-four hours and wouldn't be back until tomorrow, but Max didn't mind the wait. It would take him at least that long to recover from their little get-together by the river.

Max had told himself so often that he was in control, he had actually begun to believe it. He had believed it right up to the moment her body touched his. When he felt her firm flesh beneath his fingers, when he felt the immediacy of her, the lie had been exposed in a way he didn't like remembering.

That kind of thing wasn't going to happen again, he assured himself. It couldn't. If he was going to pull this off, he had to go slowly. He had waited a long time to have her back in his life, and he wasn't going to screw it up by letting his body run roughshod over his brain.

"If you're planning a bank robbery, I'd better warn you—old Mr. Bradley is armed."

Max turned and found Annie's redheaded friend standing on the sidewalk a couple of feet away. "Carly, isn't it?" When she nodded, he smiled. "Aren't most bank guards armed?"

"Mr. Bradley isn't the guard, he's a teller. He's also blind as a bat, feebleminded, and eager for action."

"Thanks for the warning." He glanced around. "Where's a good place for lunch?"

"New Orleans," she replied instantly. "But if you're in a hurry, Olsen's makes the best barbecue around."

"I like barbecue." He raised one brow. "Join me?"

She stared at him for a moment, openly assessing him, then nodded. "Sure, why not?"

Olsen's had the same rustic atmosphere that was cultivated by barbecue places everywhere—wooden tables flanked by long benches polished by constant use; barbed-wire collages and rusty plows hanging on rough-wood walls. The serve-yourself food was also familiar. Cole slaw and potato salad, pinto beans and hot peppers, to accompany the hickory-smoked, carefully blackened meat of your choice.

Allowing Carly to lead the way, Max carried his plastic tray to a table. After taking a bite of each item on her plate, the redhead raised her head, met his eyes squarely, and said, "Okay, so what did you want to know about Anne?"

He laughed. "I like your style. Clean. No distracting curlicues to it."

"I've been called blunt," she admitted without shame, "but I like getting to the point . . . which you aren't doing."

"Okay, what can you tell me about Annie's boss?"

"Cliff?" She shrugged. "There's not much to tell. He's a widower. Emily's leading citizen. Local-boy-makes-good kind of thing. Some people think he's on the brink of entering politics, but I doubt it. Twenty-five years ago he left with a little bit of money and came back with a lot. People here respect him for that. For his business acumen. And for the way he uses his money."

"He's a philanthropist?"

"Something like that," she said, and as they ate, catalogued the good deeds perpetrated by Annie's employer. She told Max about all the people in the area Cliff had helped. Quietly, with no flourishes, no publicity.

When she had finished, she leaned back against the wall and studied him. "But that isn't the kind of information you're looking for, is it? You want to know about Cliff and Anne. And since I won't be betraying any confidences, I'll tell you. Anne sees Cliff as a father figure. She says he's the sort of man her father should have been. And Cliff? You'll have to ask Cliff about that, but I'm pretty sure he feels the same way the rest of the town feels about Anne."

"Little Orphan Annie? Tinkerbell? Clap your hands if you want to keep her alive." When Carly frowned, he added, "I'm not being sarcastic. It's fairly obvious they all love her. You can see it in their faces when she simply passes them on the street."

Carly gave a wry smile as she shook her head. "She thinks they're just being kind to an outsider."

"People are always being kind to Annie," he said, pronouncing the words carefully, without inflection.

Carly wiped her mouth with a paper napkin,

and after folding it neatly, she laid it across her plate. Then, with deliberate movements, she placed both forearms on the table and leaned toward him, her expression casual, her eyes hard. "I don't know what you're up to, but you'd better know right now that a lot of people around here would be *very* unhappy if Anne got hurt."

Max laughed. He hadn't meant to, but he couldn't help it. "No . . . no, I'm not laughing at you," he said, still chuckling as heat rose in her face. "It's just that she warned me too. She told me in so many words that I'd better not mess with her town. The only difference is she didn't sound like a Mafia hit man when she said it." He paused and smiled. "I gather you and Annie are close."

"She's my best friend, my one true friend. She's the only one who sees exactly who and what I am. And she thinks that's okay," Carly explained, her voice husky as she gave a helpless shrug.

"That sounds like Annie. Having a prostitute for a mother made her extra sensitive to—" He broke off, and stared at her. "You didn't know, did you?"

She looked stunned as she shook her head mechanically. "I wish you hadn't told me," she said, her voice low, almost angry. "No wonder she doesn't talk about her childhood. No wonder she thinks the people here are wonderful simply because they like her. Judas priest, how do you get over something like that?"

"You don't," he said with a grim precision. "It influenced her in ways even she didn't realize."

The redhead abruptly slid to the end of the bench and rose to her feet. "Thanks for lunch," she said without looking at him "I hope you enjoy your stay in Emily." Then she was gone.

Tough lady, Max thought minutes later as he walked out of the café. Tough and very protective.

Carly's attitude toward Annie didn't come as any great surprise to Max. He had seen it too many times before. As a matter of fact he had once felt the same way himself. Annie looked vulnerable, fragile. But looks could be deceiving. Max had helped raise her, and he knew better than anyone what she was made of. Nothing less than tempered steel ran through Annie's backbone.

When they were growing up, her strength had shown itself in the way she stood up to bullies. And no matter what Max did, there were always bullies to remind Annie that she was the daughter of a whore. But she never let them see they had the power to hurt her. She kept her back straight and her head high. And she refused to let them see her cry.

Max would never forget—could never forget—the night he had discovered that, of the two of them, she was stronger. The night they had first made love.

It had all started on a night in early February. He, Annie, and Ellie had been together as usual. Mr. Bright was working the night shift, so they had assembled at Ellie's house, sprawling around on the living-room floor as they played anything-goes blackjack.

"Hit me again," Annie said.

Max, the dealer for this particular hand, paused as he pulled a card off the top of the deck. "I've already hit you five times at least. You're bust, Annie. Admit it."

"Not necessarily," Ellie said, shifting her long legs to a more comfortable position. "You forget we're going for forty-eight instead of twenty-one."

Max rolled his eyes. "Who made up this stupid game?"

"I did," Anne said, grinning. "I call it This Time Annie Wins. So hit me again, Max."

"Are we getting kinky?"

The three of them glanced up as Max's younger brother strolled into the room. Roger Decatur had brown hair, a round face, and was several inches shorter than Max. Although he was nineteen, Roger almost never acted his age.

"I always wondered what you three did in here," he said as he moved closer. "What's this, S-and-M poker? Who's hitting whom?"

"Get lost, Roger," Ellie said without looking away from her cards. "This is my house, and no one invited you in."

Ignoring her, Roger reached down and pulled a lock of Annie's hair. "How about it, Annie? Strip down and I'll give you a spanking."

Max rose slowly to his feet. He didn't say anything. He didn't even more toward his brother, but Roger stared at him for a moment, then threw up his hands and made a big production of backing away from Annie.

"No need for you to work up a sweat, big brother," he said. "I just came over to tell you our dear old aunt isn't too pleased that you decided to keep your old job instead of taking the one they offered you at the car wash. The way she sees it, you're cheating her out of ten more dollars a week. She's talking about kicking you out."

Max shrugged. "So what else is new? I don't suppose it ever occurred to you to get a job so you can help out with the bills?"

"Me? You gotta be kidding. Aunt Charlotte doesn't expect me to work. I'm the college whiz kid, remember? The one with the bright future." He smiled in satisfaction. "I can't waste my time at a job."

"How can you be like this?" Annie asked, her delicate features showing confusion. "Max is only staying in that house because he feels responsible for you. How can you stand by and let your aunt take his paycheck and give it to you for spending money?"

Ellie gave a loud snort. "Because he's a brown-nosing, two-faced pig who has the personality of a slug and the potential of a burnt match. And if I weren't such a kindhearted person, I'd mention his looks and his breath."

When Roger took a step toward Ellie, she merely laughed. After a moment Max laughed too. "You'd better watch out, Roger. If it comes to a fight, my money's on Ellie."

Roger swung on his heels, saying, "I'm not

wasting my time on some old bag of bones." At the door he looked back over his shoulder. "But any time Annie wants to wrestle, I'll make time. What are you charging now, Annie?"

Max literally saw red. He let out a roar of rage, but before he could reach the door, Annie had wrapped herself around him, and Roger was gone.

"It doesn't matter, Max," she said, her voice raised so she could be heard over his swearing. "Let him go." She clasped his face between her hands and turned his head toward her. "Don't you see? It's the only way he could get at you. He knows you're better, a million times better, than he is, and hurting me is the only way he can hurt you." She smiled. "But it didn't hurt. So he loses again. Okay?"

He stared down at her, caught anew by her beauty, by the sweetness of her soul. "You shouldn't have to put up with garbage like that. And that it should come from my own brother. It just—"

"Pisses you off," Ellie finished for him. "Roger generally has that effect on everybody."

They all laughed then, and the tension in the room eased. But moments later Max noticed that Annie was unusually pale. "You look tired, honey. You're not over that cold yet, are you?"

"I'm fine, Max," she said. "You've got to stop trying to baby me."

Reaching out, he touched her face with gentle fingers. "I just don't want anything to happen to you."

Ellie made gagging sounds. "If we're getting to the mushy part now, I can leave the room."

Max stood up and pulled Annie to her feet. "Stay where you are. It's time for me to take Annie home."

Overruling her objections, Max made Annie put on his leather jacket. They left the house by the back door. He always took Annie home by way of the alley. She would climb in her bedroom window, and Rose Seaton, habitually busy with other things, would never even know her daughter had been out.

When they reached her yard, Max pulled Annie into his arms without speaking, and he heard her sigh an instant before his mouth claimed hers. The few minutes before they said good night was the only time Max allowed himself the luxury of holding her. Keeping his hands off Annie was difficult enough without adding the complication of very intimate caresses.

"Okay, that's enough," he said, the words a rough whisper against her soft, warm neck. "I want you to get to bed."

"You're bossy," she said, pretending to pout. "I'm not a little girl anymore."

"I know that. I just don't want you to have bags under your eyes when I take pictures of you tomorrow. It would ruin all my shots."

Leaning forward, she bit his chin, then kissed the same spot. "Just a minute more, Max?"

"Not a minute, not a second." He turned her around and swatted her behind. "Go on, get to bed."

Making a stirrup of his hands, he boosted her over the rickety wooden fence. A moment later he heard her drop to the other side. Then in a loud whisper, she said, "Max . . . catch!" just as his jacket fell on his head.

"Thanks," he muttered.

He heard her smothering a laugh. "I do love you, Max. So much. Good night."

" 'Night, squirt," he said, then turned to walk back toward Ellie's house to say good night.

Ellie was waiting for him at the back door, her arms full of Annie's schoolbooks.

"I could drop them off tomorrow morning on my way to work," the brunette offered.

He shook his head. "I'll take them to her now. I don't think her mother will hear me."

"Her mother wouldn't notice if the Battle of Little Big Horn were being fought in Annie's room," Ellie said dryly. "It's after ten. That means she's been sloshed for at least three hours."

Mrs. Seaton's drinking was another thing for Max to worry about as he walked down the alley. Rose Seaton's "friends" were there at all hours of the night, and the rest of the time she was drunk.

He hated the thought of his sweet Annie having to live in that house. It always amazed him how she had learned to survive in such an atmosphere. But she did more than survive. Like a delicate butterfly floating above a battle-ground, she somehow managed to keep herself separate from the carnage.

In a few months she would graduate from

high school. Then next year she would be attending Southern Methodist University on a full scholarship. His Annie would be with normal people. She would see what life could be like for someone as bright as she. And by the time she got her degree, Max would be established as a photographer. Then they would get married, and together they would travel to every exotic, unknown place that struck their fancy. She would be beside him while he captured the world on film.

It was a plan he and Annie had discussed a thousand times. When things got tough, they talked about "someday," that time in the future when they wouldn't have to say good night at a dilapidated fence. That "someday" when he didn't have to worry about her every minute of the day and night. In that wonderful "someday" Max would know she was safe, because she would be with him. Forever.

When he reached her backyard, Max pitched the books over the fence, then pulled himself up and over. He was halfway across the yard when he heard her scream.

Throwing the books down, he broke into a run, his mind numb with fear. When he finally reached her window, he found it locked. Not hesitating, he picked up one of the bricks that lined her flower bed and heaved it through the window.

As he reached in to unfasten the catch, he saw her. And he saw the man who held her, the man who leaned against her as he stared open-mouthed at the glass on the floor. Annie's white blouse was torn across the shoulder, and her long hair fell across her face as she struggled wildly.

The following few minutes would always be a blank for Max. He only knew that when he returned to awareness, he had Annie's attacker pinned to the floor. Annie was screaming at him as she tried to pry his fingers loose from the man's neck, and Mrs. Seaton stood in the doorway, swaying as she called Max every foul name she could think of.

Max didn't give a damn about Rose Seaton, but when he saw the petrified look on Annie's face, he reluctantly released the man's throat and pushed off him.

Catching Annie in his arms, he turned toward her mother. "I'm taking her with me," he said, his voice hoarse and tight with barely suppressed rage. "She won't spend another night in your house."

"I'll have you arrested!" Mrs. Seaton screamed. "I'll have you charged with kidnapping . . . with *statutory rape*! It'll be a long time before you see the light of day, you little punk."

"Try it," Max ground out. "You don't know what trouble is, lady. You try and stop us, and I'll be the one to call the police. Or didn't you know they throw whores in jail?"

"Max," Annie whispered, her eyes pleading.

Pushing past her mother, he took Annie out the back door, and when he reached the fence, he simply kicked the rotten gate off its hinges. He could feel Annie shaking against him, and it ripped him up. She wasn't crying—Annie never cried—but she wouldn't stop shaking. Not even when they reached the lighted safety of Ellie's house.

Half an hour later, after Ellie had taken her fury out on the living-room furniture, brought Annie a clean blouse, and made her a hot drink, the brunette looked across the kitchen table at Max. "What are you going to do? She can't go back there."

"She's not going back. I'm going to marry her," he said quietly. The thought of that bastard touching Annie made Max sick to his stomach. It couldn't happen again. He wouldn't let it happen again. "We're getting married," he told Ellie. "Now . . . tonight."

"Max, we can't," Annie said, looking up from her cup. It was the first thing she had said since he had dragged her away from her house. "You can't marry me just to get me away from my mother."

"Don't be an idiot," Ellie said, her voice blunt. "Even my father, who barely knows what day it is, knows that Max loves you."

Annie rose abruptly to her feet, shaking her head vehemently. "It'll ruin everything for you. We were going to wait until I finished college. Until you had trained with a real photographer. You said—"

"Forget what I said. Do you want to marry me or not?"

Giving him a helpless look, she whispered, "It's all I've ever wanted."

He rose to his feet and gave her a quick hug.

"So what are we arguing about?" He glanced at Ellie. "You coming with us?"

The brunette laughed. "I'd be real flattered at the invitation, Max, except that you and I both know your old Yamaha wouldn't make it to the next town, much less across the state line. You're after my car, aren't you?"

"Please come with us, Ellie," Annie said. Max relaxed a little when he saw excitement and pleasure bring the color back to her face. "You can be Max's best man, and maid of honor for me."

After leaving a note for Mr. Bright, they took Ellie's car and headed for Mexico. On the way Ellie and Annie sang every song they had ever heard, making up the words when memory failed. Max was subjected to a dozen different versions of "Going to the Chapel." It drove him crazy, but he listened without complaint because anything was better than seeing the helpless, hopeless look in Annie's beautiful gray eyes.

They were married the next day, and immediately after the wedding they headed back to Dallas. Ellie slept in the back while Annie sat next to Max, close, as though she didn't want so much as an inch between them.

Darkness had fallen by the time they left Ellie at her house and took his motorcycle to a motel on the interstate highway. The Hi-Vue Motel, straight from the set of a slasher movie, had only half a dozen units. The outside walls were painted a sickly shade of turquoise, a fact that went largely unnoticed because most of the lights by the doorways were burnt out. It was the least charming place Max had ever seen. But it was all he could afford.

Gritting his teeth, he unlocked the door to their room, picked Annie up in his arms, and carried her across the threshold. Seconds later he set her abruptly on her feet and looked around.

The inside was worse than the outside. The tiny, square box had a musty-attic smell, the curtains had been stapled to the windows, and the bed sagged in the middle. There wasn't even a television set.

"This wasn't how I planned it," he said tightly. "I wanted it to be perfect for you. There was supposed to be sand and sea and music playing on steel drums."

"It's not so bad," Annie said as she moved around the room. "It's clean and the lock works. And look . . . we even have our own bathroom. Give it a chance, Max. It grows on you. In fact I'm beginning to think it's kind of cute."

He gave a shout of startled laughter. "You're crazy."

She shook her head. "No," she said as she crossed the room and wrapped her arms around him. "You're the one who's crazy if you think 'perfect' has anything to do with sand and steel drums. 'Perfect' is being married to the man I've loved all my life. 'Perfect' is having your arms around me. Knowing you love me back, that's 'perfect.'"

He caught her face in his hands and stared down at her. "You are the most precious thing in my life," he choked out. "You hear me? I don't know what I'd do without you. You anchor me, Annie. You make me real."

When she pulled his head down, pressing eager lips to his, Max forgot all about the sagging bed and the stapled curtains. In the past there were times Max thought he would go out of his mind with wanting her. And now he had her. Everything—the dreary room, the frustrations of the past—was forgotten the moment he touched his sweet Annie.

Picking her up in his arms, he carried her across the room. When he reached the bed, he looked down at her and muttered, "Cute?"

She began to laugh, and when they dropped together to the bed and automatically rolled to the middle, she laughed even harder. And as Max laughed with her, he knew she was right. This was perfect.

He lay beside her, holding her, and began to make plans for their future. "And since I won't be living with Aunt Charlotte, my paycheck should be enough for now. We won't be able to afford a big apartment, but I bet we can find something. Ellie will help us look. I can keep up my photography at night and on the weekends. The newspaper will take whatever I get to them, and I told you about that regional competition I'm going to enter. If I can place in that—"

He broke off when he realized she hadn't spoken in quite a while. "Are you tired, baby?"

"No," she said slowly. "I'm not tired. I'm not sleepy. I'm married."

Recognizing the wry note in her voice, he

drew back his head to look at her. "What a coincidence. So am I."

"I'm new at this," she continued as though he hadn't spoken. "It's the first time I've ever been married, but I've heard rumors. And somehow I got the silly idea that on a honeymoon, in their honeymoon bed, the people involved did more than talk." She glanced at him, one brow raised. "Now is a fine time to tell me you're only interested in my mind."

He met her eyes. "I rushed you into marriage, Annie. I just didn't want to rush you into anything else. I can wait until—"

"I can't," she broke in, shaking her head. "I'm less noble than you. Or maybe I'm greedier. Needier."

"No, not needier," he said in a husky whisper as he picked up her hand and placed it against his heart, letting her feel how it pounded at her nearness. "I'm just afraid of doing the wrong thing. I want the best for you, Annie."

"I have the best," she told him. "Right here beside me. Right here in my arms."

As he watched her warily, she moved away from him. With confident movements she unbuttoned the borrowed blouse, shrugged out of it, and dropped it to the floor. Seconds later her bra joined it.

Annie wasn't talking anymore. But she was smiling. She was smiling a narrow-eyed, secretive smile as she pushed up his shirt and brushed her breasts lightly, oh so lightly, against his bare chest, letting him see the way the nipples hardened for him.

There was no holding Max back then. He would have fought an army to get to her. All the joy from his past, every hope for his future, were combined in the small woman in his arms. The woman who was freely, joyfully giving herself to him.

Making love with Annie took his breath away. There was no shyness, no hesitancy in her at all. Even when he knew he was giving her pain, she wouldn't let him stop, wouldn't let him slow down. Max knew he was giving her pleasure—he could see it in her eyes—and she wasn't stingy in returning the favor. She held nothing back. She gave every bit of herself to him. With single-minded determination she had reached out and grabbed happiness with both hands.

That night Annie had needed no one's protection, Max thought as he unlocked the door of his rented car and slid inside. And she still didn't. She was still stronger than anyone— man, woman, or child—Max had ever met. But she had everyone in this town fooled. Annie was good at that too.

As he pulled the car out into traffic, Max wondered if her good friend Carly knew that the day Annie had walked out on him, only three months after their wedding night, she had left with another man.

Six

The doorbell rang as Anne stepped out of
the shower. She scrambled into her robe and
tripped twice on the dangling sash before she
reached the living room.

It's not Max, you dope, she chided silently,
forcing herself to slow down before she broke a
leg. It couldn't be Max. She and Cliff had only
just returned from Houston. Max couldn't possibly know that they were back.

"So how did it go?" Carly said when Anne
opened the door.

Anne stared at her friend for a moment, then
shook away the disappointment. "Do you have
spotters on the road?" she asked, her voice dry.
"We got in only an hour ago."

"Christie Graham was visiting her Grannie
Jean out on Airport Road," the redhead explained as she followed Anne to the bedroom.

"When she saw you and Cliff drive by, she called Jess Gibb, Jess called Lovey St. John, and Lovey called Mama. So how did it go?" she repeated, and flopped down on the bed next to the open suitcase while Anne returned to the bathroom to dress.

"We got two, 'I'm sorry but' and one 'Let me think about it and get back to you,'" Anne called through the open door. "But he won't. Get back to us, I mean. He was just too nice to say 'I'm sorry but' to our faces."

After pulling on her jeans, Anne poked her head around the door. "Are those new boots?"

Carly extended one long leg to give her a better look. "I got them in Fredericksburg last week. Tell me how much you love them."

"I love them."

"I said tell me how much. They were expensive . . . gush a little."

Anne considered the extravagant footgear in question. "I love them more than chocolate pudding but not as much as Mel Gibson, and I'm envious as hell because Western boots always make me feel as if I'm wearing Clementine's boxes without topses. Where's Petey-oh-Petey today?" she threw over her shoulder as she ducked back into the bathroom.

"Out at the farm with his cousins. They're going to bottle-feed the new calf today. I told him I'd drive out there as soon as I talk to you."

"You mean you took a chance on missing your turn just for me?" The words were muffled through the pink sweatshirt Anne was pulling over her head. "I'm touched. I really am."

Carly laughed, then in an odd little silence fell between them. After a while Carly said, "I had lunch with your ex yesterday."

Anne slowly put down her hairbrush and stared at her face in the mirror. She had been trying not to think about Max, trying and failing. Turning away from the mirror, she walked back into the bedroom. "Did you?" she said, keeping her voice casual.

"Yup. He took me to Olsen's. Anne . . ." Carly slid off the bed and stood up. Moments later, as though reaching a difficult decision, she met Anne's eyes. "I think your Max is up to something, Anne. He took me to lunch so he could pump me about you and Cliff."

"That's not unusual, is it? I mean, I'm curious about him too." She grinned. "It's too bad he didn't bring a talkative friend along."

"I wasn't that talkative. Mostly PR stuff for Cliff, but . . . there was something there, under the surface that I couldn't put my finger on. The man has a lot of charisma, and he knows how to make a woman pay attention."

Anne laughed at the wariness in her friend's face. "You mean he's sexy as hell. You're not exactly telling me anything I didn't already know."

"Yeah, well," Carly began, shifting in discomfort. "He may be sexy, but he's also deep. Deep men make me nervous. I still say he's up to something."

"Max is a complicated man," Anne said slowly. "He was eleven years ago, and now . . . A lot can happen in eleven years, and experience always adds extra bits and pieces to your personality. But that doesn't mean he's up to something. His mind was probably on his work when he was talking to you. Max always gets moody about his work."

After a moment Carly shrugged. "Okay, I done my duty. If he murders you in your sleep, don't say I didn't warn you. And now I'd better go catch up with Master Petey. If I'm lucky, that calf will be fed, burped, and put down for its nap by the time I get there."

Anne walked Carly to the door, and the red-head was getting into her battered Dodge when Max's rented car pulled smoothly into the driveway. Although Carly made no comment, she gave Anne a long, hard look before starting the engine.

Max reached the front door just as Carly backed out and drove away. "Is it something I said?" he asked, staring at the dust cloud thrown up by the retreating Dodge.

"She had to go see a man about a calf."

Anne couldn't take her gaze from his face. She had been gone less than forty-eight hours, but seeing him was like watching the sun come out after a long rain.

"How did you—" she began, then broke off, and shook her head. "No, don't tell me. Lovey called you too."

"Wrong," he said, his eyes sparkling with amusement. "She called Billy Loomis, and Billy called me. I take it you didn't get any bites in Houston."

"Billy told you that too?" she asked, cutting her eyes toward him in skepticism.

"No, I figured that one out all by myself. You and Cliff would be rounding up the city council if you had good news."

"Smart aleck," she said, laughing. "Come in and I'll make us some iced tea."

"We don't have time," he said as he took her arm and began to urge her toward his car.

"We don't? Why don't we?"

"Because once the wind dies down, we won't be able to fly the kites I found at the Mercantile."

"Kites? Good grief, I haven't flown a kite since we were kids."

"Neither have I. That's why I bought them. Remember the ones we made out of Styrofoam and tissue paper?"

She nodded, laughing. "We armed Ellie's Ken and Barbie dolls with knitting needles you had swiped from your aunt and tied them to those tacky-looking kites."

"Vicious brutes, weren't we? Talk about bloody dogfights. Come on, we only have a couple of hours, so get your butt in gear. Time, that old bald cheater, is a-wastin'. It's putting its winged chariot into third gear. While we stand here talking, old *tempus* is *fugit*ing. . . ."

She couldn't stop laughing as he dragged her to the car. "You idiot. This is March. What makes you think the wind is going to stop blowing in a couple of hours?"

"Alf Woodard said the wind will definitely die down by early afternoon."

"Why on earth would you listen to Alf?" she

asked as she fastened her seatbelt. "He's a sweetheart, but ever since that fly ball landed on his head, he's been getting weather predictions from the pigeons at the courthouse, and those dumb birds are always wrong."

This time, however, the pigeons knew what they were talking about. Anne and Max managed to get in only two and a half hours of flying time before the wind abruptly died. But it was enough.

She had beat him twice in unmanned, unarmed dogfights. "If that happens again, I may have to hurt you," Max had warned her after the second time.

Anne had laughed, running to send her kite soaring through the sky toward his.

It was a day straight out of a storybook. Never had the sky been so blue. Never had plain grass been so green. They raced each other across fields covered with unending flowers, giant patches of blue and pink and yellow. And as she stood, letting the wind whip around her, the same wind caught his laughter and carried it across the field to bathe her in the wonderful sound.

And finally when, as the pigeons had foretold, the wind subsided, they dropped down, exhausted, to lie on the cool, soft winter grass and talk in lazy whispers.

"I haven't asked where you're living now," she said after a while. "In Texas?"

He had been propped up on one elbow, a long stalk of grass between his teeth. Now he rolled onto his back and stared up at the sky. "In

Texas," he confirmed. "And in California . . . Indonesia . . . Venezuela. Everywhere and no- where. That's why I'm driving a rented car. No place to park one." He closed his eyes. "I can't seem to settle in one spot. I like them all. So I just go where the wind blows me."

"Like little Japanese islands?"

He turned back to her, cushioning his head with his folded arm. "You know about the time I spent in the Ryukyus?" When she nodded, he said, "I stayed there longer than anywhere else. It was a strange place. Time skips right over those little islands. The people live exactly the way their grandparents and great-grandparents did." His brown eyes suddenly took on a gleam of amusement. "Remember during our Tarzan phase when I tied a rope to the chinaberry tree in Ellie's backyard and we pretended it was a jungle vine?"

"Are you kidding? Of course I remember." Tarzan had come after the Three Musketeers and before Superman. Max, being the only one willing to bare his chest, took the role of Tarzan.

"Ellie got to be a gunrunner and a jungle warrior and an evil queen," she said, "but you left me up in that dumb chinaberry tree."

"Where else would Jane stay?" he asked, grin- ning.

"What made you think of our Tarzan games?"

"Well," he said slowly as he tickled her chin with the stalk of grass. "On my little Japanese island there were real jungles. Real vines."

"You didn't," she said, laughing in disbelief.

"Didn't I? I'd only been there for a couple of

weeks when the villagers took me with them to gather fruit. When I saw those vines—they were hanging everywhere—I couldn't resist." He laughed. "I went through the whole bit. Standing on a limb, beating my chest. I even did the yell. My island friends got a big kick out of that."

"How did it feel? Was it as wonderful as we imagined it would be?"

"It was wild. Fighting gravity and the wind. It made me feel powerful . . . until the vine broke. I cracked a bone in my foot when I landed. Then I picked up an assortment of scratches and bruises on the trip back to the village because my buddies were laughing so hard, they kept dropping me."

Anne had started laughing even before he got to the end. "I wish I had been there to see it," she said, still shaking with laughter. "I wish I had been there to *do* it. I would have done a better job."

"Sure you would," he said, openly skeptical. "You couldn't even stay in that stupid chinaberry tree for half an hour without falling. I never could figure that out. You didn't fall when you were the imprisoned queen, but you were a lousy Jane."

"I didn't fall out when I was queen because I was terrified of heights. I was afraid to move." She gave a soft laugh. "I sat hugging the limb for dear life until I heard you and Ellie coming back. Then I would pretend I was right at home up there."

"Why didn't you tell me that you were afraid?" he said, frowning.

She shrugged. "I don't know. I guess I was even more afraid that you and Ellie wouldn't play with me anymore. Anyway by the time I became Jane, I was used to heights and I got braver." She grinned. "While you and Ellie were out fighting jungle wars, I was practicing on the vine. And I was better than you. I *never* landed in the azaleas."

When he raised a threatening fist, she laughed. "You should have taken a picture of yourself—Maximilian Decatur, wounded apeman—and included it in your last book. I loved those pictures. One of them, the one that you took of that wrinkled old fisherman, reminded me of another of yours. He was a fisherman, too, but he was Mexican. Do you know which one I'm talking about? They didn't resemble each other physically, but there was a certain look in the eyes of both. Serenity. Or maybe it was endurance. It was as though they had both discovered some secret about life that the rest of us won't or can't seem to grasp."

"That photograph—the one of the Mexican fisherman—that was never published," he said slowly. "How did you know about it? When did you see it? *Where* did you see it?"

She glanced away from him. "Six years ago at the Atlanta exhibit."

A frown cut deep grooves in his brow. "They were only on display for a week, and I was there every day."

"I know. I saw you," she said, keeping her voice light. There was no reason for her to explain why she hadn't made herself known to him. They both knew why.

"I was there on opening night," she continued. "Oh, Max, I was so proud of you that night. Everyone in that swank gallery recognized what I've always known. That you're the best there is."

After a moment of taut silence, he drew in a slow breath and smiled. "You may be exaggerating just a little bit."

"No," she said softly, then, raising her hand to shade her eyes against the sun as she watched a bird in flight, she added casually, "How long were you with McNeal Reynolds?"

"A little over two years. We traveled all over the world, seeing all those places you and I used to talk about." He gave a short laugh. "I was so ignorant back then. I thought I could just go out and take pictures, but McNeal showed me there was a lot more to it. He taught me about dealing with people. He taught me to prepare. I studied history and politics and languages. And before we went to a place, we went through tons of pictures that had been taken there in the past, because McNeal knew you can't recognize a fresh angle until you know what's been done before. He showed me techniques that would have taken me years to learn on my own."

"And he got you noticed," she added slowly.

"He got me noticed," he agreed. "His endorsement opened all the right doors. Working with McNeal was the opportunity of a lifetime, and I never felt like I made him understand how much I appreciated the chance." He paused, staring up at the sky. "You heard that he died a few years ago?"

She nodded. "Yes, I read about it. I was sad of course, but I couldn't help thinking that it was somehow providential. Not his death, but the fact that he stayed in the world just long enough to help you polish your gift. It was almost as though he had chosen you to take his place."

Letting her head fall back to the grass, she smiled. "I'm glad he got that chance," she said softly.

Max stared down at her, taking in the fragility, the delicacy of her features. And for a brief moment he wondered why she was so interested in the time he had spent with McNeal Reynolds. Then, shelving his curiosity, he stretched lazily and closed his eyes.

Today had been good. He had forgotten what it was like to be young. He was only thirty-three, not so old, and he still had most of his life ahead of him, but there had been times in the past eleven years when that didn't seem like such a good thing.

Annie thought she owed him something; he had seen acknowledgment of the debt in her eyes on his first night in Emily. Giving him back a little of his youth wasn't a bad beginning.

And now, lying beside her on the grass, he looked back into the past, trying to pinpoint the exact time when he had lost the ability to stand in the sun and laugh, when he had lost his openness to life. He only knew the process had begun the day he came home to find Annie gone.

But he couldn't think about that now. He couldn't let the past clutter up his thoughts and feelings. He had to look at the two of them as a man and a woman who happened to enjoy each other's company. He had to convince himself of that truth. Because if he was going to have any kind of peace in the future, he had to make this work.

He had worked hard today to put her at ease. He wanted her to get past the self-conscious stage, and he was relatively sure this little field trip had accomplished that, but it hadn't been easy on him. In all the planning, in all his calculations, he had never taken into consideration how tough it was going to be to keep his hands off her.

His stupidity was almost laughable. The sight of her sent his pulse racing, and now, when she was close enough for him to feel the warmth, when he caught the perfumed scent of her hair, he was damned lucky he didn't start baying at a nonexistent moon.

And there was no use in telling himself that it would have been the same with any attractive woman. He had already tried that and it didn't work. He wasn't a deprived man responding with unthinking hunger to an attractive woman. It went deeper than that. Much deeper. As he always had, and probably always would, he was responding to Annie.

Anne smiled as she studied the changing expressions on Max's face. She could watch him every minute of every day for the rest of her life and never grow tired of it. It was amazing that ordinary bones and muscles and flesh came together in such an extraordinary way.

This day with him had been pure joy, she thought, closing her eyes. For a little while she had managed to disregard reality. The reality of what had happened in the past. The reality of what might happen in the future. Today the turmoil in her mind and heart had retreated to a bearable distance.

It had retreated, but it hadn't disappeared. It was still there, inside her. It was always there.

Just like the monster in the closet, she thought with a drowsy smile.

The year that Anne turned six, a monster had come to live in the closet of her room in the house on Weiden Street. During the day the monster didn't bother her. She felt free to get clothes or shoes or toys from her closet, because she knew without being told that the monster went somewhere else in the daytime. But when the sun went down and shadows filled the room, it always came back. She knew it was back because she would hear the floorboards move beneath its awful feet. Too many nights she had lain awake with the covers pulled over her head, trembling uncontrollably as she waited for it to finally come and get her.

And even when she didn't hide her head and shake, even when she had other things on her mind and managed to forget about the thing in her closet temporarily, a feeling of anxious dread always lingered on the edges of her awareness.

Anne lived in fear of the monster until the day

she grew strong enough to open the closet door in the dead of night. In the simple act of confronting it, she had destroyed it.

The outcome had been predictable; childhood monsters were notoriously tenuous creatures, but the monster Anne lived with now, the same one she had lived with for the past eleven years, was made of more solid stuff. And even on a day like this, this wonderful, fantastic day that Max had given her, the beast was in her mind's closet, waiting impatiently to get at her.

"Come out, come out, wherever you are," Max said softly.

She glanced up at him and smiled. "Sorry, I was daydreaming. Did you say something?"

"Nothing important. Just that there's a ladybug in your hair."

"Where?" She raised her hands to her hair. "Don't let me squash it. Which side?"

"Hold still. You're not even close." He leaned over her, his face close to hers as he gently separated strands of her hair to free the trapped insect.

"You know, your hair is the most amazing stuff," he said, his voice slightly distracted. "In the shadows it looks like someone spilled strawberry jam in the honey, but when the sun hits it, the colors damn near come alive."

"Strawberry jam?" she said, laughing. "Is that a line you use often? Because I have to tell you . . ."

The words died away in her throat as his warm breath on her face and the fingers threading through her hair sent shivers of awareness through her body, as though his nearness was in itself a caress.

"You have to tell me what?" he prompted.

She swallowed, then gave a breathless laugh. "I forgot what I was going to say but . . . but I'm almost sure it was something pithy and to the point."

Get a grip, she told herself as she fought to control the involuntary reactions. Babbling certainly wouldn't help anything.

"There, got it." He lowered his hand to show her the tiny red creature crawling on his extended index finger. "Safe and sound."

When it reached the tip of his finger, the ladybug flew away, but Anne barely noticed. He was so close.

"Little Annie," he said softly.

Leaning down, he brushed his lips across hers, once, twice, then a third time. A breathless moan caught in the back of her throat. The sensations that had been so strong moments ago became explosive. Every inch of her body tingled with aching awareness.

Her muscles tightened; then, a second before she arched her body toward his, he patted her cheek and sat up.

"Come on, squirt," he said, grabbing her hand as he stood up and pulled her to her feet. "If we stay here any longer, the dew will start settling on us."

She blinked twice, her mind blank, her heart racing. He was smiling at her. It was a warm, friendly smile. So why did she feel as though he'd just pulled the rug out from under her? Why did she feel that there was something, deep in those sable-brown eyes, that should make her want to turn and run?

Seven

Anne arranged with Cliff to take a week off. It would be a while before their next trip, and she wanted to free up her time, in case Max wanted her to show him around. And miraculously that was just exactly what he wanted.

Throughout the next few days they were together constantly, and although she used part of that time to introduce him to her friends and neighbors, more often than not he forgot about his project and lured her into simply having fun—canoeing on the river, country dancing at the Longhorn, driving to Fredericksburg to look at antiques.

And bit by bit Anne realized the vigilance—the overactive awareness she felt in his presence—was beginning to disappear. She knew she was being worse than foolish, but as the days passed, Anne began to actually believe that it was possible for the past to disappear. It was as though she were being given a chance to rewrite her history with Max. And this time there were no stumbling blocks, no terrible decisions to make. She came to believe that this time it might work.

With a physical effort, she pushed the past aside and allowed herself the luxury of being close to him without fighting her reactions. There was no need for her to fight, because he wanted to be with her as much as she wanted to be with him. She could even touch him without the nagging certainty that she was about to make a fool of herself.

Not that she didn't still want him. She did, more than ever. But she no longer fought her responses. When they danced, she didn't hesitate to press her body close to his. And when they kissed, she wasn't afraid her instant, unflagging reaction would embarrass him.

Being with Max felt natural again. And she knew that if he took it a step farther and made love to her, their coming together would feel just as natural.

But it didn't happen. As the week progressed, as the kisses and caresses became more frequent, Anne kept telling herself that this time it would happen. But as though he held an invisible measuring stick, when a certain point was reached, Max always pulled back, teasing her, joking with her until her emotional temperature returned to normal.

This was the state of affairs when, a little over a week after Max showed up in Emily, the third member of the Weiden Street trio joined them: Elise and her husband, Garrick, flew in from Dallas to spend the day with Anne and Max.

Ellie was even more beautiful than Anne remembered. At first the brunette's exquisitely polished looks were intimidating, but it didn't take Anne long to realize that beneath the polished exterior Ellie was still Ellie.

While the men went fly-fishing, Anne and Ellie spent the afternoon catching up on each other's lives, trading secrets just as they had done when they were kids. And later, while Max and Garrick went to town to fetch bread and wine, she and Ellie worked together to prepare dinner.

"Aren't you glad we stayed cute?" Ellie asked, her tone smug as she and Anne pulled salad ingredients from the refrigerator.

Anne raised a questioning brow. "Did we really have a say in the matter?"

"Of course we did." Ellie stood at the sink and began washing the vegetables. "I don't see why I should share credit with my genes. How many strands of DNA do you see in aerobics classes? Or making an appointment to get encased in mud?"

"Okay, okay." Anne laughed. "I'm glad we decided to stay cute."

"Oh, my gosh, I forgot to tell you," Ellie squealed, her eyes brimming with laughter as she turned to Anne. "Guess who I saw last month? Sandra Jo Whittaker."

They had both known Sandra Jo in high school, and anyone who had ever met Sandra remembered her. She had platinum-blond hair, wore tight sweaters, and filed the heels of her shoes so she would walk like Marilyn Monroe. Anne and Ellie had spent most of their high school years envying Sandra Jo Whittaker.

Anne rolled her eyes. "Don't tell me. She's married to a millionaire and rides around town in a chauffeured limousine, nodding to the peasantry as she passes by."

"Wrong," Ellie said. "She married a widower with three children, then they had two of their own. And guess what he does for a living? He's a minister. I kid you not, Annie, Sandra Jo Whittaker married a minister. She has brown hair now, and she's as pudgy as all get out. And here's the kicker—she's *sweet*."

"I don't believe it," Anne gasped. "Not Sandra Jo. Max used to send us ahead of him so we could check and make sure she wasn't waiting to ambush him. She did everything except climb into his bed when he wasn't looking."

"She would have done that, too, if she thought she could get away with it. Remember the time she started dating Roger? Roger was so conceited, he never even guessed that she was using him to get closer to Max." Ellie shook her head ruefully. "The college whiz kid. He was so sure he would be important, and he winds up with a string of used-car lots."

Anne laughed. "Is that what he's doing now? Actually that doesn't surprise me. Roger could talk a hole through a brick wall."

When silence fell in the room, Anne glanced up to find Ellie watching her closely. "You didn't know what Roger is doing now? You didn't know that he's married, has two children, and lives in Phoenix?"

Switching her gaze back to the sink, Anne turned off the water. "No," she said quietly, "I didn't know any of that."

After a moment Ellie said, "Annie, why did you run off with Roger?"

The question caught Anne off guard, and she stood at the sink trying to formulate, not an answer but some polite equivocation that Ellie would accept.

Ellie, however, wasn't going to wait around for an evasion. "Just the idea of it made me uncomfortable. Still does, as a matter of fact. You and *Roger*." Ellie made a face. "I remember that you were nicer to Roger than anyone else, but I always thought that was simply because you were so polite, so blasted *good*. But then when you left with him—"

The brunette broke off, and shook her head. "It messed me up for a while. Being so monumentally wrong about you made me question everything I believed in. Like maybe there were a lot of things I was wrong about."

"I'm sorry," Anne said quietly. "I didn't realize. People talk about the ripple effect, but you never think you could be the one to set the waves in motion." She met Ellie's dark eyes. "You've obviously forgiven me, and I thank you for that. It means a lot to me."

Ellie shrugged. "There's nothing to forgive. It was a decision you had to make on your own. Anyway the damage to me was relatively minor."

Glancing away, Anne began stripping leaves

off the lettuce head. "You mean compared with what I did to Max?" she said, keeping her voice even. "I know I hurt him, but—sometimes it's better for everyone concerned if the end is quick and final. When something is wrong, it's . . . it's *cruel* to let it drag out, to let the wasted time build up until you're overwhelmed by regret and thoughts of what might have been."

"You mean if you had stayed with him, without loving him, he would have been hurt worse? I suppose that's possible," Ellie said doubtfully as she nibbled on a carrot. "But I'm afraid if you had told me that eleven years ago, when Genna Reynolds was pursuing him so avidly, I would have called you a liar. I would have said anything was better than seeing Max get tangled up with her. Even being stuck in a bad marriage." She rolled her eyes extravagantly. "Darling Genna was so smug, so pleased, that he was free of entanglements, as she called it. I met her only a couple of times, you understand, but I'll tell you flat out, the woman gave me a bellyache."

"Did he—Did Genna get what she wanted?" The question came out before Anne could stop it. As she carefully avoided Ellie's eyes, she added, "I didn't like her . . . and when I heard Max was working with McNeal, I wondered."

"At the time I wondered too," Ellie admitted. "Max has high standards, you know that. But he was hurting quite a—I'm going to be blunt, Annie. You knocked the stuffing out of him, and for a couple of years, when he would fly in for a visit, I saw him go through hell. I honestly didn't know whether or not he was going to pull out of it. I was afraid he would let Genna sucker him into playing her little games. She certainly looked like she could do things for a man's ego. But Max had too much respect for McNeal. Even if he had wanted Genna, which in retrospect I don't think he did, he wouldn't have done that to McNeal."

"I'm glad," Anne whispered, letting out a slow breath as she felt the tension in her ease. Then, glancing up, she found Ellie studying her face.

"You and Max haven't talked about it? I mean, about your leaving and how he felt about it?"

Anne shook her head. "I tried to bring it up a couple of times. I really did try, Ellie. But when he acted as though it didn't matter, I realized it was better this way. Because the truth is I don't have anything to say. I can apologize for doing it the way I did, but I can't say I made a mistake. All I could say is, our marriage was a mistake, so I left. And he knows that already."

"You made a mistake with one brother so you thought you would try it with the other? Did you give Roger three months too?"

The blunt words sent blood rushing to Anne's face. "I—"

"No, don't answer," Ellie said, shaking her head. "It's none of my business. I was just trying to show you that there are still things you and Max need to talk about."

Anne closed her eyes for a moment, then turned to look at her friend. "I'm afraid, Ellie," she whispered. "Opening that closet door scares me to death. No, I know that doesn't make any sense. It's just that the past few days have been like . . . it's as though all these years I've been buried alive, with the full knowledge that I was going to spend the rest of my life there. Then a miracle happens and I'm allowed to step out into the sunlight. I just want it to last a little while longer. That's not too much to ask, is it?" she asked, hating the pleading note in her voice.

"No, it's not too much to ask." Although Ellie's voice was soothing, her eyes were worried. "But sooner or later it's going to come up. And I'm very much afraid it will be worse for you when it happens." She drew in a slow breath. "Which brings me to one of the reasons I wanted to see you. This whole situation between you and Max has me worried. Max is not the same person we knew back on Weiden Street. He's changed, Annie. A lot."

Anne nodded slowly. "So have I. So have you. It's part of life."

"Sure it is, but with Max it's not that simple. I guess the best way to show you what I mean is to tell you about the women in Max's life."

"No . . . no, don't," Anne said, shaking her head vehemently. "That's something I don't want to know about. Ever."

"Don't be stupid. I'm not going to list them or tell you what they did together. I'm not even going to tell you how he felt about them. But if you step back and look at the whole, you can see what kind of changes I'm talking about. At first, for over a year after you left, there was no one. That bothered me. He was so totally alone. I was scared for him. Then suddenly he started having affairs right and left. And he seemed to deliberately look for the worst sort of women. The ones who play sophisticated, destructive games. The ones who use and discard, use and discard. Only Max would always beat them to the punch. I guess it gave him some momentary satisfaction. And now . . ." She shrugged. "Several years ago he stopped playing the games, he stopped having affairs. As though he had proved some obscure point and now doesn't need anyone."

She met Anne's eyes. "I love Max, Annie, but I don't have any illusions about him. There's something warped inside him. In the eleven years since you left him, he hasn't had one close relationship with a woman. He's turned into a hard, cynical man."

Anne studied her friend's face for a moment. "Are you trying to warn me against Max?"

"I don't know," Ellie said, shaking her head. "I guess I'm afraid for both of you. You've both been hurt enough. I don't want it to happen all over again."

Anne smiled. "You're a good friend, but you're looking at this all wrong. You mistakenly believe that this thing between Max and myself can be stopped. It can't. What I feel, what I want, makes no difference. It has to unravel in its own time, in its own way."

Then before the brunette could continue the discussion, Anne glanced down at her watch. "They'll be back soon. Can you finish the salad while I change into something a little more festive?" She smiled. "It's not every day that the three of us get together."

"Annie . . . no, never mind. Go on and change your clothes."

In the bedroom Anne pulled a sage-green handkerchief-linen dress from the closet. The dress was one of her favorites, but she didn't wear it often. It was old-fashioned and softly feminine; there was nothing gung-ho executive about it. But tonight she was Annie rather than Anne. So tonight it was perfect.

She brushed out her hair, clipping it loosely at the base of her neck, and had just stepped out of the bedroom when the men returned from town.

By the time they had finished eating dinner on the terrace, it was dark, so Anne served their coffee in the living room, listening to the other three talk as she moved about the room.

Ellie's husband wasn't a talkative man, but he had a dry sense of humor that tended to take one off guard, and when he made a contribution to the conversation, it was intelligent and to the point. At first Anne was afraid they were excluding Garrick with all their "remember when" talk, but he seemed to genuinely enjoy watching his wife enjoy herself. And as Garrick and Ellie sat together on the couch, the brunette would, without a pause in her speech, occasionally pick up her husband's hand and hold it against her cheek in an unconscious caress.

Their closeness, their unity of spirit, was obvious, and although Anne was glad for her friend, she felt a strange, unexplainable little sadness settle over her.

• • •

"But it's not that late," Anne said as she and Max walked the other couple to the door. Although it was after midnight, Anne simply wasn't ready for the night to end.

"Not if you live in China," Ellie said, yawning noisily. "But in Emily, Texas, it's definitely late. And if we don't get going, Joe Mack might give Number Ten to someone else."

Anne laughed and said her good-byes. While Max walked them to their car, she began gathering up the cups and saucers, humming softly as she worked.

"What are you thinking about that makes you hum so sweetly?"

Anne glanced over her shoulder and saw Max leaning against the wall behind her. She smiled and said, "You know very well that I can't carry a tune. I was thinking about tonight, about the three of us being together again. During all the years we were apart, I knew I was missing you both, but for some reason I felt the loss more keenly tonight, when we were together. Does that make sense?"

"Sure it does. It's like being in the dark for a long time. You feel a general kind of funk. Then, when the sun comes out, you can pinpoint exactly what it was you were missing."

He reached out and took the cups and saucers out of her hands. "We can do this later." Setting the dishes aside, he pulled her down to the couch beside him. "What did you think of Ellie's old man?"

"I liked him." She smiled. "Garrick obviously adores her. How could I not like a man with such good taste?"

"It hasn't all been smooth sailing for them. They met when she was Miss Hotshot Model, so she figured he was attracted to Elise Adler Bright instead of plain old Ellie, but I think it was the tiny pieces of Ellie that he saw and fell in love with. He was just as bad. He thought his scarred hand made her queasy and that she was just putting up with him because he was good in the sack. At least this is what I gathered from the little Ellie told me. They were on the verge of divorce just last year."

"But they seemed so close tonight," she said, frowning.

"They've worked hard at getting to this point. Sometimes telling the truth about your feelings seems like going into a riot without wearing a flak jacket." He smiled his inward-turned smile. "Sometimes you can't even tell the truth to yourself."

She stared at his somber features. "Max—"

"What did you and Ellie talk about while Garrick and I were out doing man-type things?"

She pushed the hair back from her face, her thoughts distracted. "What? Oh, nothing really. We talked about old times . . . and Sandra Jo Whittaker and"—she dropped her gaze to the hands that were clasped in her lap—"we talked a little about you being here in Emily. I think Ellie's worried about us. I mean, about the two of us being together . . . not *together* together, but—"

"I know what you mean," he said, laughing as he put his arm around her and pulled her close. "Ellie thinks I've turned into a cold, heartless man. Did she warn you to guard your back?"

"Something like that," she admitted with a rueful little smile.

"I hope you told her to mind her own business."

Rising to her feet, she walked to the fireplace and stood with her back to him. "No, I told her it didn't matter if you had ulterior motives. I told her it didn't matter because I couldn't stop this from happening even if I wanted to."

She sensed his presence behind her just moments before she felt his hands at her waist. "By 'this' do you mean this"—he touched his lips to the side of her neck—"and this"—he slid his hand up to cup one firm breast.

Her head dropped back to rest on his shoulder; her heart pounded violently. Moaning, she turned in his arms and kissed him, deeply, urgently, her tongue seeking his.

Then suddenly he was doing it again. He was pulling away, talking as though he were picking up a conversation that had been briefly, inconsequentially, interrupted.

"Next time they come, we should take Ellie over to Fredericksburg," he said, stooping to pick up the clasp that had somehow fallen from Anne's hair. "She's a real nut for atmosphere."

Watching him, she pushed a trembling hand through her loosened hair. "Is this part of it, Max?" she asked, her voice rough with frustration. "Is it part of the plan? Just give me enough to get me stirred up, then pull back?"

He stared at her for a moment with narrowed eyes. "Are you stirred up, Annie?" he asked softly.

"Oh, yes." She gave a shaky laugh. "I'm not afraid to admit it. I would have admitted it that first night at the Longhorn if you had asked. So where does that get us, Max? I'm not complaining, you understand. I just want to know what the rules are? Or is that part of the game plan? Take away the rules, just to keep me off balance. Well, you've won. I'm off balance. And I repeat, where does that get us?"

He raised one brow. "You sound annoyed, Annie. It's been a long day. You're probably tired."

She drew in a slow, steadying breath and raised her gaze to his face. There was confidence there. He was sure of her. And he had a right to be. She was in for the duration, and they both knew it.

Moving closer, Anne rested her hands on his shoulders. He still watched her, but now his dark eyes were wary. "Ellie was right, wasn't she?" She brushed a kiss across his chin, then the corner of his mouth. "These past few days you've been suckering me in. Is it pay-back time, Max?"

He reached up to grasp her hands, holding them between their bodies to keep her from moving closer. "Ellie has seen me a couple of times in the past six years. She knows *nothing*," he said, his voice harsh.

Anne pulled her hands loose and pushed closer, moving her body against his, feeling his warmth through the soft linen of her dress. "She said you haven't had a woman in quite a while. It must be tough on you, being this close."

"You don't know what you're doing," he ground out, and there was a warning in his voice.

"Don't I?" She took his hand and held it to her breast. "In your heart you may despise me," she whispered. "In your mind you may feel contempt for the woman who left you and ran away *with your own brother*, but your body hasn't got the message"—she slid one hand up his thigh—"has it, Max?"

"*Damn you.*" With one movement he had her on the couch, her body pinned firmly beneath him, his face inches from hers. "Damn your soul to hell. You want it now? Fine, we'll do it this way. Contempt? Sweet heaven, that's a pitiful emotion compared with what I feel for you, Annie. Do you know what it was like, do you have any idea how it felt, knowing you were with Roger? Knowing my own brother was touching you, making love to you." The words came out in a tight, unrelenting stream. "And damn your lying eyes, it didn't go away. The image didn't fade with time." He gave a short, fevered laugh. "The gift that keeps on giving. You can't imagine all the nights during the past eleven years that I've lain awake thinking about what I would do to you when I found you again."

His face was even closer now, and she not only heard his words, she felt their heat on her face.

"I loved those nights, Annie. Planning how I was going to make you pay became my greatest source of pleasure. I never knew I could be so creative. I thought of a thousand different ways to make you suffer. And in my fantasies I savored your pain. I saw you go down on your knees and beg for mercy."

He threw back his head and drew in a deep, ragged breath. "It was better than sex, Annie," he whispered hoarsely. "Better than any drug ever invented. The sheer pleasure of it would leave me shaking all over, the way I'm shaking now. Feel me shaking, Annie. I'm shaking because I know the reality is going to be even better than those dreams."

When he paused, as though waiting for a response, Anne simply stared at him, her eyes wide as the pain spread through her body. But it wasn't her pain she felt. It was his.

Frowning, Max grasped her chin between his forefinger and thumb, holding her still, trying to claim even more of her attention.

"This isn't the way it was supposed to be," he rasped out, his throat raw with anger. "As soon as I saw you in San Antonio, I started making plans. I followed you here . . . you didn't know that, did you? I planned it so carefully. And I wasn't going to take more than my share. No, I wanted the end, the grand finale, to be fair and equitable. An eye-for-an-eye kind of thing. I was going to wait until you came to depend on me for your happiness, the way I had depended on you. Before we reached this point, you should have needed me so desperately, you would be able to see no future without me. Exactly the way I needed you." As he talked, Max watched her face with avid, hungry interest. "I wanted to wait until you reached the peak of happiness. And when you thought life couldn't get any better, when you thanked God every minute for sending me to you, when every breath you took exhilarated you, simply because you knew I was in your life, that was when I was going to rip every dream you ever dreamed to shreds, Annie." His fingers trembled on her chin. "Just as you did to me."

He rested his forehead against hers, drawing in several short drafts of air as he tried to steady his thoughts, his words, his hands.

Seconds later he drew his head back a couple of inches so he could see her again. It was important that he *see* her. "But you screwed up the plan. That's all right. I can still make it work."

Without taking his gaze from her face, he eased his body off hers just enough to get his right hand to the front of her dress.

"I can still make it work," he repeated as he opened the top button. "During eleven years of sleepless nights you tend to do a lot of thinking. And one of the things I thought about was the way I treated you back then."

He worked the next button loose. "I treated you like an innocent. Like a fragile, porcelain doll that might break with rough handling. Roger, now, he had a more realistic approach. He treated you like a second-generation whore."

Max gave a harsh laugh, and another button

slipped free. "My little brother taught me a lesson there, I can tell you. Did you stare at the ceiling and grit your teeth when I made love to you? You should have told me back then, Annie. We could have worked something out. I admit at the time I was a little naïve, but you don't have to worry about that now. I've run into a few, shall we say, *bent* appetites since then. I'm sure I can give you just exactly what you need."

He unfastened the last button and pushed the fabric to the side. "You see? Nothing here to inspire such awe in me. It's just a body. A beautiful body agreed, but certainly not hallowed ground, the way I thought back then. An instrument of pleasure, that's all you were to Roger. And as you can see, I've come around to his way of thinking."

As he unfastened the clasp on the front of her silk bra, Max fought again to keep his hand steady, but his strength was giving out. "Why aren't you saying anything, Annie? I always figured you would fight. I figured a struggle would make it more interesting for you."

His breath was coming in ragged gasps now, and he could barely hear his own words over the pounding of his heart. "That's all right," he said in a rough whisper. "You don't have to do anything. Just lie back and enjoy it. You are enjoying it, aren't you, Annie?"

He captured one smooth breast with rough fingers, squeezing, manipulating. With his other hand he explored her body with coarse caresses, caresses designed to hurt and humiliate. And as he touched her, he watched her face.

Now! The word was a scream inside his head. Now it was time for him to feel the rush of satisfaction. Now it was time for him to feel the heady triumph he had always known would come to him at this moment.

But it didn't happen. There was no satisfaction, no surge of triumph. And as he continued to stare into her gray eyes, he knew there would be none.

Without saying a word, without striking a blow, Annie had won again. She had defeated him with sadness. How could he have forgotten that when Annie was sad, the look in her eyes could twist a grown man's insides?

A weary shudder shook through him, and with mechanical movements he began to pull away from her.

Annie blinked twice, then again, as though awakening from a dream. "What are you doing?" Her words were a hoarse, barely audible whisper. "Finish it, Max. Damn you, *finish it*!"

She caught one of his hands and pressed it brutally against her naked breasts. "Second-generation whore . . . remember? Do it, Max. Pull up my dress. Here . . . here, I'll do it. Come on, Max, where's your guts? Screw me. Do whatever it takes to finish this once and for all. I'm ready for you, Max." As the frantic words poured out of her, she moved her body against him. "Let's get it all out in the open, so you can stop hating me. So I can stop hating myself."

"Stop it." He jerked his hand away from her heated flesh and pushed away from her. "Stop it, Annie."

As he moved to sit at the end of the couch, his body twitched spasmodically with leftover rage, leftover passion. He heard the dry sobs shake through her body, but Max had no comfort to give her. He had none to give himself.

Max wasn't sure how much time had passed before he stood up and pushed a rough hand through his hair. She still lay on the couch, her eyes wide as she stared at the ceiling, but Max didn't speak to her. He didn't even say good-bye as he walked out of the room and out of her house.

Anne leaned against the tiled wall of the shower, letting the cool water flow over her. She had been in the shower for over half an hour, but she wasn't trying to wash away his touch. She was trying to wash away the sadness, the hopelessness.

There had been so much anger and pain in him. For eleven years it had been growing and spreading. The force of it had shocked her, knocking her sideways with its brutal intensity.

After drying off, she pulled on a robe and left the bathroom. She passed the bed and kept going. She wouldn't sleep tonight. It would be a long time before she would sleep again. The house that had always brought her comfort now seemed to echo with his angry words. His hatred for her permeated the walls and furniture.

Outside, on the terrace, she sat in a wide chair and wrapped the robe more securely around her body, trying to get warm, but the terry-cloth robe didn't help because the chill wasn't in the air. It was inside her. How did one go about warming a soul?

For hours Anne sat staring into the darkness, and there was only the faintest lightening in the sky when she heard footsteps on the flagstones. Although she hadn't expected him to return—she hadn't expected ever to see Max again—Anne felt no surprise. Maybe she was beyond feeling any emotion as benign as surprise.

She heard his slow movements as he sat in a chair a few feet from her, but she couldn't seem to turn her head away from the birth struggles of the new day.

"I was mad as hell when I left," he said without preamble.

She leaned her head back and laughed, inaudibly, mirthlessly, at the understatement.

"I told myself that you had won again," he continued. "It took me a while to understand it wasn't what I saw in your eyes that stopped me. You didn't do it to me again. I did it to myself. Looking into your eyes simply made me realize that if I got rid of the anger, I would be left with nothing. For eleven years all I've had to keep me going was the need for revenge. I set no other goals for myself. After hurting you, what came next? Just a whole lot of nothing." He exhaled a deep, ragged sigh. "I've played my last card, Annie. So what in hell am I going to do now?"

Still staring straight ahead, she said, "I suppose you could always serve it up in smaller portions . . . to make it last longer."

He gave a dry laugh. "No, planning revenge

kept me going. It vitalized me. At times I think it kept me alive. But carrying it out? No, I don't have the strength for it. I don't have the stomach for it."

She moved her head against the puffy cushion. "It's been a night for revelations," she said softly. "Like you, I learned things about myself tonight. When you showed up in Emily, it was like . . . it was like someone put a light in the window for me, so I could find my way home. It seemed you had put the past behind you, where I, on the other hand, had definitely not. I believed that if you said the words, if you said, 'I forgive you, Annie,' then all the bad would just go away. We would be friends again, and I would be able to get on with my life, maybe even start a family." She exhaled a slow, weary sigh. "We're a sorry pair, Max. A truly sad pair."

"Do you still want me to say the words?"

The quietly spoken question made her glance at him for the first time since he had walked onto the terrace. After a moment she shook her head. "No, that was my revelation. Tonight I realized that nothing is going to make it go away. Nothing you could do to me will make me feel I had paid for what I did, and no words will give me absolution. I'm afraid this is Carly's old Flying Fickle Finger. 'The moving finger writes; and, having writ, moves on . . .'" she quoted softly. "There's nothing either of us can do to cancel out what's already been written. But I'm glad it's out in the open now. I don't have to spend all my time being afraid of what might happen." She gave a breathless laugh. "It happened, and it's every bit as bad as I thought it would be."

He shifted with a restless movement. "So where does that leave us?"

"Worse off than when we started, I'm afraid. You thought revenge would make you whole again, and I was betting heavily on forgiveness. Now neither of us can say, 'When this happens, everything will come right again.'"

He stood up. "'Sorry pair' is an understatement," he said, his voice dry. "I tell you what, Annie, I don't think we're fit company for anyone else. We'd be smart to just stick to each other."

Her heart gave a little jump. "What do you mean?"

"It wouldn't be fair to pull anyone else into this 'grim and comfortless despair' we're wallowing around in, right?"

She swallowed heavily. "Well, yes, you're probably right about that, but I hadn't exactly . . . I mean, there are no hordes of men who will be devastated by that decision."

He chuckled, a sound she found both delightful and shocking. "You said you wanted to get on with your life. You said you wanted children. I'm ready for that too." He sat down and rested his forearms on his thighs as he leaned toward her. "We've agreed that we're doomed to be miserable, so why don't we do it together?"

She raised one skeptical brow. "When did you come up with this brilliant scheme?"

"Just now." He grinned. "Pretty good for the spur of the moment, don't you think?"

She shook her head. "A lunatic . . . a raving lunatic. And I'm *listening.* 'By a knight of ghosts and shadows/ I summoned am to tourney/ Ten leagues beyond the wide world's end./ Methinks it is no journey.'" She shook her head again. "Out of your freaking mind."

"What was that from?" he asked, smiling. "I liked it."

"You would. It's 'Tom o' Bedlam,' probably a distant relative of yours . . . or mine." She raised her eyes to his. "It's not that I want to be a party pooper, but a couple of small items seem to have slipped what's left of your mind—you hate me . . . and I'm pretty well terrified of you."

"So there are a few problems," he said, moving his shoulders in a dismissive shrug. "All new relationships come with kinks that have to be ironed out."

She laughed. She leaned back in the chair and laughed long and hard, and after a moment he joined her. "Come on, Annie," he said finally. "At least think about it. Like it or not, there are ties between us. Ties that have survived eleven years of separation. Eleven years of anger and pain and guilt."

When she didn't respond right away, he reached out and picked up her hand. "Okay, let's look at this from another angle. Suppose you met me for the first time tomorrow. You'd be attracted to me, wouldn't you?" He turned his head to the side. "Look at this profile. Have you ever seen better bone structure? I still have all my own teeth. And just between the two of us, I make a bundle. So what's not to like?"

She shook her head. "Mr. Humility. Yes, Max, if we met for the first time tomorrow, I would definitely be attracted, but—"

"Well, there you go," he said in triumph. "And if I met you for the first time tomorrow, you can bet I would be in hot pursuit within minutes. So why don't we do that?"

"Do what?" She pulled her hand loose and stood up, pausing for a moment to reknot the tie of her robe.

"Why don't we meet for the first time tomorrow—no, right now, because it's already tomorrow." He rose to his feet and stood in front of her. "Hi, I'm Max Decatur. I'm famous, and I think you're cute as all get out."

"I can't believe this," she muttered, shaking her head. "I'm actually standing here, wondering if we can possibly make this work. That's crazy. A few hours ago you hated me so much, you were shaking with it."

"I didn't know you then," he said, moving closer. "A few hours ago I was all tangled up in the bitterness I felt for a girl I once knew. I hated my ex-wife . . . maybe I still hate her, I don't know, but that has nothing to do with us. I want to get to know *you*. Don't you want the chance to get to know me?"

God help her, she did. She wanted that more than anything on earth. But it couldn't possibly work. Could it?

At that moment the sun's light fought its way free of the trees across the river, and the world came alive around her. And, standing in the brilliant light, Anne made a decision. She wouldn't go back to the shadows without a fight.

She turned her head and met his eyes. "Hello, Max," she said slowly. "I'm Anne."

Eight

Two days after Anne and Max made their extraordinary agreement, Anne went back to work. Max's suggestion. She was to get back to the job of helping Cliff rescue Emily, while Max continued with his project, the project that had begun as a pretense but now held his interest. He said they needed to take the holiday atmosphere out of their relationship. He said they needed to see if they could fit into each other's everyday lives. What Max said didn't always make sense, but in this case Anne thought he might have a point.

Anne's emotions were split down the middle. Part of her was certain she was participating in a harebrained scheme that didn't have a snowball's chance in hell of working. A scheme conceived by a lunatic, aided and abetted by an even bigger one. But another part of her shoved sanity aside and began making room for the new man in her life. Her step was lighter, the air more intoxicating, and she couldn't wait to finish work each day so she could be with Max.

She took him to meet her special friends. She watched him fall under the spell of Lacey Cobb, the old woman with the Romanov face, and she laughed as he swapped tall stories with Mr. Hayes. She shared Emily with him and watched him gradually fall in love with her town.

Some nights they went out and sampled Emily's nightlife, and sometimes they prepared dinner together and ate on the terrace or in her small dining room. Although he always left her by ten, he usually called and kept her on the phone until well after midnight. During their conversations they didn't cover any subjects of earth-shaking importance. It was simply a general sharing of thoughts and ideas.

One Saturday, almost two weeks after they made what Max called their cracked pact, they sat at the kitchen table finishing lunch as she told him about the trip she and Cliff were taking early the next week.

"I'm worried about Cliff," she said, talking through a mouthful of chocolate cake. "He seems tired all the time. No matter what he says, this project is taking a lot out of him." She raised her glass and swallowed the last of her milk. "He's not supposed to be working full-time."

"Then why does he do it?"

"Because he's the most loyal, giving man I know," she said softly.

Max stared at her for a moment. "Don't you think you go a little overboard in the hero worship? Every other word out of your mouth is about Cliff."

The undisguised sarcasm caught her by surprise. "Don't you like Cliff?" She frowned. "You don't really know him, do you? The two of you haven't even had a chance to talk. Why don't I invite him over for dinner one night, then the two of you can—"

He shoved back his chair with an abrupt movement and stood up. "Don't go to any trouble on my account. I don't have to like him. He's your boss, not mine." He walked to the back door. "I think I'll take a walk by the river."

She stared in bewilderment as the door closed behind him. He had sounded angry. No, he had sounded jealous. Although the idea struck Anne as slightly ridiculous, she remembered that Carly had also thought there was something between Cliff and Anne. And she had to admit it wasn't an ordinary employer-employee alliance. She couldn't expect Max to automatically understand how she felt about Cliff.

She caught up with him a quarter of a mile from the house. He was sitting under a tree, his knees loosely drawn up as he tossed rocks into the water.

"I should have explained about Cliff before," she said without preamble. "I'm sorry. My only excuse is that I take my relationship with him for granted. I forget that other people might think it's a little . . . peculiar."

She paused, gathering her thoughts. "What I'm going to tell you is not designed to elicit sympathy. I want you to know that up front. I just want to show you, I want you to understand how I feel about Cliff."

Anne leaned with her back against the tree. She couldn't look at him because talking about that time in her life made her uncomfortable.

"After I left—No, let me start over." She cleared her throat. "Soon after I turned eighteen, I found myself alone in the world and decided to move to Houston. There was no reason really. It was a big city, and I thought I could find work there. That was probably a mistake. You see, I didn't have a high school diploma or any kind of work experience. I was qualified for nothing." She drew in a slow breath. "Anyway, like thousands of others I ended up on welfare. It . . . it wasn't fun. I was treated with contempt or pity or just plain indifference, and of the three I preferred the contempt. It wasn't as debilitating, it wasn't as diminishing, as the other two. Luckily after a couple of months I landed a job at a factory, making plastic lamps."

She hesitated, remembering the crushing loneliness, the mind-numbing fear of those distant days.

"Where was Roger?"

The bluntly spoken question took her by surprise. She turned her head to stare at him, her brow creased with confusion. "I thought we weren't going to talk about—"

"Forget that for a minute," he said, his voice abrupt. "Where was Roger?"

"Didn't you talk to him . . . when he got back to Dallas?"

He glanced away from her. "I haven't talked to Roger since the week before you left."

"Oh, I see. Well . . ." She gave a nervous laugh. "Things didn't work out for us."

"How long did you stay together?"

"Not long," she whispered, then she cleared her throat. "Anyway, to get back to what I was saying, after I got the job at the factory, I rented a place of my own." She smiled. "Actually it was only one little room, but it was better than the homeless shelters. And then, after a while, I enrolled in a couple of business courses at the community college. I was naïve enough to think that once I had completed the courses, I would be able to get a better job, a job with some kind of future."

"But it didn't work out that way?"

She shook her head. "There was always someone more qualified, someone with experience or a list of degrees or both."

"Where does Wariner come into this?"

"I met him purely by accident. I was working two jobs by that time. I was still at the factory at night, but during the day I worked as a waitress. It wasn't what you'd call a top-drawer establishment, but the food was good, and occasionally businessmen came in for lunch. On this particular day Cliff was there with his wife, Paula, and while they looked at the menus, they talked. Paula was saying that they should invent a loyalty test. She was in a real snit because Cliff had trained two assistants only to have them leave to take executive positions with other companies."

Anne gave a soft laugh. "I don't know what got into me. I was standing there waiting to take their order, and before I knew what was happening, I said, 'I'm loyal.' Paula looked as though the chair had suddenly started talking, but I just kept going. I told them I was loyal and honest and they wouldn't find anyone who worked harder. Then suddenly I was sitting down at the table going over the training that I had had, assuring them that I would take whatever classes they wanted me to take. Paula was trying to get the manager's attention, but Cliff was laughing. And after he had quieted Paula down, he gave me his card and told me to come see him when I got off work. Then he ordered the chef salad."

"And the rest, as they say, is history," Max said.

"As they say," she agreed. "Paula and I became good friends, and if anyone says Cliff could find a better assistant, he's lying. I've made sure I was the best."

She glanced at him. "I'll never forget what Cliff did for me. If it weren't for him, I wouldn't have my beautiful little house. I wouldn't have my friends here in Emily. I probably wouldn't even have met you again." She paused, then said quietly, "And that would have been my biggest loss."

He stood up and caught both her hands in his. "Please accept my most sincere and humble apology, O great and magnanimous Anne."

She smiled. "I thought that was supposed to be magnificent."

"You are most definitely magnificent," he said, his voice husky. "But I hope you're also feeling a little magnanimous, and that you'll forgive me for acting like a first-class jerk."

She shrugged. "We're just getting to know each other. These things happen in any new relationship."

He laughed and, releasing her hands, began to walk with her toward the house. Anne had known he wouldn't continue holding her hands. He had barely touched her since the night they had had their memorable encounter in her living room. Anne didn't know what to think of that. In a way she was glad they were taking things slow. Using restraint decreased their chances of making a mistake. But on the other hand, the lack of physical contact was like a wall between them. They were both so very much aware that they *weren't* touching, and she was afraid that the longer they waited, the more difficult it would become to breach that wall.

And that was why Anne decided, with a cool head and a clear mind, that it would be better all the way around if she seduced Max.

"The fire feels good, doesn't it?" Anne said lazily. "It's a little chilly tonight."

It was the night before she was due to fly to Atlanta with Cliff. Anne and Max had finished dinner half an hour earlier, and now they sat in the living room, she on the couch, he in an armchair, as they drank cognac in little bubble-shaped glasses.

Anne, working on instinct and ideas picked up from late-night movies, had set the scene carefully. She wore a silk dress that floated on the air when she walked and clung provocatively when she was still. Dinner by candlelight had seemed too obvious, but she had turned the dimmer switch in the dining room to its lowest setting. And as stirring love songs played in the background, she had taken every opportunity to brush against him, holding his attention with meaningful pauses and long, lingering gazes.

The result of all her extraordinary effort was that Anne was thoroughly aroused. Excited. Stimulated. She was damned hot. Hot and moist and ready.

And Max? Max was talking about the plans he had made to watch *Saturday Night Wrestling* with Mr. Hayes.

Abruptly tossing back the rest of the cognac, he stood up. "Well, I guess I'd better shove off," he said as he leaned down to put his glass on the coffee table.

"It's not ten yet," she said, patting the couch beside her. "Come sit here and tell me who you photographed today."

He eyed the couch warily. "No . . ." he said, drawing the word out. "I don't think so. I don't care much for that couch." He met her eyes. "What do you think you're doing, Anne?"

Exasperated, she let out a puff of air and rose to her feet. "I'm trying to seduce you, and since it's perfectly obvious that I'm bad at it, the least you could do is pretend not to notice. Don't you know anything about civilized behavior?"

He had started laughing with her first words, and by the time she finished, he was holding her in his arms, rocking them both with his laughter.

"Poor baby," he said, still chuckling against her neck. "Want me to teach you how?"

"Yes, please," she said without hesitation.

He laughed even harder then and pulled her down to sit on the rug in front of the fire. "How old are you anyway?"

Giving him a suspicious look, she said, "I'm twenty-eight . . . why?"

"How did you get to that advanced age without learning—" He broke off and carefully examined her face. "How long has it been since you made love, Anne?"

She frowned. "What kind of question is that? I thought you were going to instruct me in the fine art of seduction."

"We'll get to the seduction later. Now answer my question. How long has it been?"

"Well, give me a minute," she said in irritation. "It's not like I keep a record." She glanced away from him. "Let's just say it's been a while."

"No, let's not say that. Let's say exactly how long. Months?" he prompted. "Years?"

"Months . . . years," she said, looking down as she picked at the pile of the rug. "But you don't have to feel sorry for me. I've had plenty of offers. They just never worked out."

After a moment of silence he said, "How many years?"

She met his eyes with an exasperated sigh.

"You are so stubborn. Okay, it's been over ten years. Is that exact enough for you?"

He whistled softly and turned his head to stare into the flames. The silence that drew out interminably began to make her nervous.

"What are you thinking about?" she asked finally.

"I was thinking that you're pretty amazing. And I was wondering if your abstinence was some kind of self-inflicted punishment for . . . for something in your past." He turned his head and met her eyes. "And I was thinking that you didn't miss much. During the ten years you were sleeping alone, I wasn't. And it was lonely, Anne. It was damned lonely. After a while it sickens your soul. I'm glad you were smarter than I was."

Blinking away unexpected tears, she picked up his hand to lay it against her neck, then she turned it slowly and pressed her lips to the rough palm. "You should have more delicate hands," she murmured huskily. "Artists aren't supposed to have blacksmith hands."

When she touched her tongue to the palm of his hand, he sucked in a sharp breath. "Lady, you don't need any lessons," he said in a rough whisper. "Do you know what else I was thinking?"

"There's more?"

"Oh, yes," he said with an uneven laugh. "This is the part that got the old heart pounding. I was thinking that if you've gone ten years without loving, you're either a medical anomaly, the only human being in history without physical needs. Or . . ."

"Or?" she prompted, her voice husky.

He turned his hand to curve it around her neck and began to slowly draw her toward him. "Or you're a time bomb waiting to explode."

"Tick . . . tick . . . tick," she whispered.

He closed his eyes, drawing in a deep, ragged breath. "Ahh, love," he murmured, "now comes the part that scares me more than a little. I've wanted you since the day I saw you in San Antonio, but there was always a darker side to the wanting. I managed to hold back because I was working on a hidden agenda. The agenda's gone now. And if I let go, now that there's nothing between us except—"

"Your clothes," she whispered. "My clothes . . . and a lot of foolish talk. Are you afraid you'll scare me with a display of unbridled passion?" Her eyelids drifted down, and she watched him react to her words. "Unbridle it, Max. Turn it loose. Don't hold anything—"

The last word was cut off by his mouth. The taste of him, the feel of him, had filled Anne's dreams, waking and sleeping, for most of her adult life, and his kiss triggered the explosion he predicted. Terrified that he would find another reason to pull away from her, she brought her hands up to clasp his head and hungrily sought his tongue with her own as she thrust her body close against his.

She felt the shock of her response rock through him. He groaned, a sound that came from deep in his chest, and struggled to his feet with her in his arms.

He carried her into the bedroom and set her on her feet beside the bed. Only moments later the moonlight streaming through the curtains illuminated their naked bodies.

When he lowered her to the bed, it seemed natural and right, as though they had never been apart. There was no sign of hesitancy in either of them now. They were where Fate had intended them to be, in each other's arms.

There was no past, no future. No haunting echoes of pain. There was only this moment. And nothing mattered except the overpowering need to get closer, the need to reclaim the agonizingly beautiful sensations that time and circumstance had stolen from them.

Yes, here is the birthmark on the soft, inner part of her thigh. It still looks like a butterfly. It still tastes like Maine in spring.

Here's the scar on his back. The one he got when he fell off the house. The one that felt so good when I ran my fingers or tongue across.

And even now, even after eleven years and a world of pain had gone by, he still whispered the same love words in her ear as he lifted her buttocks and slowly filled her.

It was old. It was new. It always had been and always would be. Because when they came together, there was finally honesty. Total honesty. As they moved together, the moonlight raking gentle fingers of light across naked flesh, they touched the most solid truth either had ever known. It gathered strength and rocked through them like a distant earthquake. Then the earthquake was there in the room with them, and Annie was finally home.

With his head on the pillow next to hers, Max watched Annie as she slept. He didn't touch her. He simply watched her sleep. He wanted to etch her features more deeply into his memory so that even when he closed his eyes, he would be able to picture each one clearly.

The sun had been up for over an hour, and for even longer he had been watching her. The loss of the small things, like watching her sleep, had cut Max most deeply in their years apart. The anger and pain of her desertion would take over his thoughts at night, but he'd expected that. He had even welcomed it. But the small things would come upon him unexpectedly, touching even the most ordinary parts of his life.

But that was over, he told himself. He didn't have to worry about unexpectedly missing her now. Because now she was here beside him.

Today was the day Anne was due to fly to Atlanta with Cliff. Max wasn't jealous anymore. Not after what they had shared last night. He lay beside her in bed, wanting to watch her sleeping face but needing to kiss her even more.

Softly he touched his lips to her forehead, her eyelids, and her cheek. But the time he reached her mouth, she was awake and waiting for him.

"What a wonderful way to wake up," she murmured against his lips.

Opening her eyes, she reached up to touch his

face and smiled. A look in her smoky-gray eyes nudged at something deep inside him. Something he thought was dead and buried years ago. Hope.

The feeling began as a small thing, an inconceivable idea struggling weakly to be conceived, then before he could catch his breath, it was growing and swelling, overwhelming, taking over his whole heart and mind. And that scared the hell out of him.

Max had been prepared to spend the rest of his life alone. It wouldn't have been any difficult task, because there were no requirements for being a loser. He wouldn't even have to work at it. He could just sit back and let it happen. And it would have been a nice, smooth ride. No ups and downs for a loser. Only downs. No demands, no high standards. A loser expected nothing, and that was just exactly what he got. Nothing.

For one cowardly moment, as he looked into her eyes, he wasn't sure he was ready for the struggles that went with being a winner. Because to Max, being a winner meant only one thing: loving Annie and having her love him back.

The woman in his arms could take him higher than any mortal ever dreamed of being. But, as he knew to his cost, she could also drag him through the depths of hell.

Moments later, when she whispered a kiss across the base of his neck, Max's lips twisted in a self-mocking smile. His silent debate had been nothing but a waste of mental energy. Because he would give up an arm or leg or both before he gave up Annie.

He pulled himself up to lean against the headboard, dragging her along with him, pressing her warm body to his. "I need you to tell me something."

"You sound so serious," she said, her smile fading as she met his eyes. "Are you asking Anne or Annie?"

"I'm asking you. There's something I need to know."

After a moment's hesitation she nodded. "Okay."

"Why did you leave me?"

She caught her breath, then after a moment she moistened her lips and dropped her gaze to where her hand rested against his heart. "I was so young, Max. So desperately young. And you . . . you refused to let me grow up. But please don't think I'm blaming you. You couldn't know that when I put all my faith in you, I had none left over for myself. All I had was strength once removed. Borrowed spirit." She paused. "And when I found myself alone, when there was no one there to be my foundation, that was when I had to learn how to be strong for myself. I was an expert at relying on Maximilian Decatur, but it took me quite a while to learn how to rely on Anne Seaton."

Max stared at the ceiling for a long time, then he let out a slow breath. "So one day you just decided I was stifling you and that you would get a better deal with Roger. Is that how it happened?"

"Human motives are never that simple," she

said quietly. "I made a mistake, Max. I screwed up royally. Can't we leave it at that?"

"Sure," he said, and ducking his head, he kissed her neck. "It was stupid of me to bring it up now, when you've got to get ready to go out of town. We could probably find something better to do with the time."

"Oh, yes, Max," she breathed. "Please."

Nine

Atlanta was a beautiful city. It was big and exciting but had somehow managed to stay friendly. Art, entertainment, sports—Atlanta had everything. And Anne had never hated a city so much in her life. Because what it didn't have was Max.

Every meeting she and Cliff attended was simply time that she didn't have access to a telephone. She fidgeted and fussed and rarely kept her mind on what was being said, but if her employer noticed her preoccupation, he didn't mention it. He simply carried on without her.

Anne couldn't even feel any great disappointment when, once again, the meetings proved futile. She only knew that now that the meetings were over, she could go home. She could go back to a home that was no longer a town or a house. Home was one man's arms.

Two days later, when Anne finally stood in her driveway after Cliff had dropped her off, she turned toward the house and frowned. Max's car wasn't in the driveway. She knew it was silly, but she had expected him to be at the airport to meet her. Or at least here at the house waiting for her.

She picked up her overnight case and walked to the front door, pausing to dig the key out of her purse. She had just managed to unlock the door when Carly drove up.

"So, how did it go?" the redhead asked as she stepped out of the car.

"Come in and I'll tell you about it," Anne called, then walked through to the bedroom.

By the time the redhead reached the room, Anne had the telephone receiver in her hand and was dialing the number of the Loomis cabin.

"Have a seat," she told Carly as she let the phone ring for the fifth time.

After the tenth ring Anne replaced the phone. "Have you seen Max?" she asked, keeping her voice casual as she opened the closet door. "I wanted to—"

She broke off when she saw his clothes hanging beside hers in the closet. Her knees went weak with relief, and she wanted to do something silly, like hug his leather jacket. But she simply laughed.

Carly came to stand beside her, checking out the obviously male clothes. "Something you forgot to tell me?"

"I think Max and I are living together," she said, pressing a hand to one flushed cheek.

"You think? Unless he's paying you for storage, I would say you are definitely living together." Carly paused and studied her friend's face. "You're getting in pretty deep, Anne. Are you sure you know what you're doing?"

Anne nodded, then changed her mind in midmotion and shook her head. "No, I don't know what I'm doing. And the worst part is I don't care that I don't know. That doesn't sound reasonable, does it?"

"No, but it sounds like you. At least it sounds like the way you've been acting since your Max showed up. Lately you always sound like you're on the verge of either laughter or tears."

Anne smiled. "That's because I seem to be feeling everything so much more keenly now. Max does that for me. It's like—" She broke off and moved across the room to pick up a porcelain figurine. "Look at it, Carly. Look at the delicacy of the features. Those eyes, those little painted eyes, look as though they're smiling. As though she had a secret. Touch it. See how it feels? I touch it with my fingers and I feel the texture all the way to my bones." She set the figure aside and met Carly's eyes. "It never felt that way before. It never looked that way before. Do you understand what I'm trying to say?"

Carly stared at her for a moment, then let out a soft, slow whistle. "Girl, you're in some deep doo-doo here. You idiot, can't you see that if he can get you this high, he can also knock you lower than Hades?"

"I know," Anne said, smiling again. "He's done that already. He threw me into hell, then pulled me out." She shook her head and gave a soft laugh. "What can you do with a man like that?"

"Run," Carly said succinctly. "As far and as fast as your legs will carry you. He's out of town, by the way."

"Out of town? He didn't say anything about that."

Carly shrugged. "It was apparently something that came up unexpectedly. He told me to tell you he'd call you tomorrow and let you know when he'll get back."

Anne felt disappointment jab her heart, then spread inch by inch through her body. Would she ever get over the fear that gripped her when he wasn't in her sight, the fear that she would have to go back to being without him again?

"He didn't say where he was going?" she asked slowly.

Carly shook her head. "Not a word. Just that it was unavoidable. It probably had something to do with the project he's working on."

"Probably," Anne murmured in agreement. But she wasn't sure. Something didn't feel right. Something simply didn't feel right.

Max stepped out of the car he had rented at the Phoenix airport and leaned against the door as he glanced around, checking out the Spanish-style house. It was an expensive place. An extravagant place.

He didn't want to be here, but he could see no

other way out. The thing he had seen in Annie's eyes, the thing that hit at the heart of him, uncovering long-buried hope, allowing it to take over his every waking thought, had brought him here. There was no future for them until he could make a clean break with the past.

Drawing in a slow, steadying breath, he closed the car door and moved toward the house. It was time for the first step.

The woman who opened the front door for him was as extravagant as the house. And as expensive. Smooth platinum hair brushed her shoulders, and the casual silk jumpsuit looked like the kind of thing Ellie used to model. What he could see of her face—a quarter of it was hidden by oversized, rose-tinted sunglasses—was as flawless as the rest of her.

"Mrs. Decatur?" he said.

"That's right." Her tone was just slightly defensive, as though he had accused her of something. "What do you want?"

"I'm here to see your husband. His office said he was working at home today."

She frowned. "Is he expecting you?"

Max hid a smile. "Probably not. In fact I can almost guarantee he's not, but if you'll tell him his brother is here, maybe he'll make time for me."

"His brother? There are no brothers. Roger is an only child."

Max burst out laughing, pleased to find that he still had a sense of humor. So Roger was an only child.

"He wishes," Max said, still smiling. "I'm sorry,

Mrs. Decatur, but I really am his brother Max. Aunt Charlotte raised both of us."

"You have my sympathies," she muttered. "That woman could turn powdered milk sour. I make sure I'm out of town when she comes for a visit. Way out of town. Like Greenland or Africa." She nibbled at her glossy pink lip. "I suppose you'd better come in . . . Max. And call me Julia. Not even the maid calls me Mrs. Decatur." She walked briskly down the hall, leaving him to follow. "Roger is working out by the pool. If you'll go on out, I'll get Mary to bring refreshments. Nice meeting you," she added as an afterthought just before she disappeared.

Max found the double doors that led to the pool and walked outside. He stood for a moment, taking in the scene. Two children were in the pool. Loud children. Angry children. The younger one, a boy, looked as though he was trying to drown the older one.

The man Max assumed was father to the two hooligans was beneath a striped umbrella, reclining in a lounge chair. But instead of working he was in a sound sleep.

As Max watched, the children climbed out of the pool, and the boy chased the girl around the perimeter. When they reached their father, instead of going around the lounge chair, they went over it, and Max's brother woke up swearing.

"*Lane! Dee-Dee!*" he screamed at them. "You get your little butts in the house. Now! Damn it, why can't I get a little work done without you two screwing it up? And if you think I'm taking you with me tomorrow, you can just forget it!"

His tanned face flushed with anger, he watched as the children passed him on their way to the house, then he returned to the lounge chair.

The children—the boy looked about five and his sister was probably eight—ran by Max with little more than a passing glance, their argument continuing in hissing whispers.

When the door closed behind the pair, Max began to walk toward the pool, and he had almost reached it before Roger saw him. An instant later the younger man was on his feet, staring and gasping in shock.

The years had not been kind to Roger. He had always had a round face, but now he had a body to match. And the plaid bermuda shorts he wore with a yellow sport shirt were a big mistake. He looked like a tourist who had misplaced his camera.

It was strange. Max had expected to feel a lot of things when he finally saw Roger again. And he always figured anger would be right at the top. But now that his brother was standing here in front of him, the emotion that dominated was pity. Strange.

"Max?" Roger said in a hoarse whisper.

"How you doing, Roger?" Max said, his voice easy, casual. "It's been a few years, hasn't it?" He glanced around. "Nice place you have here."

Roger was still gasping like a dying guppie, but after swallowing a couple of times, he managed to say, "What are you doing here? How did you find me?"

Max raised one brow. "If you were in hiding, you shouldn't have let Aunt Charlotte have your address. She told Ellie years ago that you were living here in Phoenix."

The maid chose that moment to appear. She carried a round tray that held lemonade in tall glasses. Roger didn't even look at her as she placed the tray on a wrought-iron table, then quietly withdrew.

"Why are you here, Max?" Roger asked, then he laughed, a gesture that was obviously difficult for him. "It's a long way to come to buy a used car. You knew I was in the used-car business? I'm doing great, Max. Really great. My profits are up like you wouldn't believe. I'm really doing great. Not that you're not. Doing great, I mean. I've seen some of your stuff . . . in a magazine, I think." He frowned. "What did I do with that thing? I meant to save it. That brainless maid probably let the kids get at it, and if she did, there's no telling—"

"Guess who I ran into a couple of weeks ago?" Max said, interrupting the unending flow of nervous talk.

Roger picked up a glass of lemonade and took a sip. "How should I know? I don't keep up with your—"

"Annie," Max said softly.

The ice rattled in the glass that Roger held in his hand. Avoiding Max's eyes, he steadied his hand as he carefully took another sip of lemonade. "Is that right?" he said finally. "How did she look?"

"Beautiful. Even more beautiful than she was

eleven years ago." Max sat down in a wrought-iron armchair. "She's a woman now. Very much a woman."

Roger wiped perspiration from his brow with the back of one hand, but he didn't comment. And he still refused to meet Max's eyes.

"You know why I'm here, don't you, Roger? We need to have a little talk. I want you to tell me about the events of one particular day. I want you to tell me about the day you ran off with my wife."

Roger darted a look at Max, and in the brief moment that their eyes met, Max recognized several things in his brother's eyes. There was sullen anger, and there was fear. And there was unmistakable, undeniable triumph. There was smug satisfaction. For that Max wanted to kill him.

Clenching his fists, he said, "Talk, Roger."

"I don't have to tell you anything."

"No," Max agreed. "You don't have to . . . but you're going to. One way or the other."

Roger turned his head to stare at him openly. "Are you threatening me?"

Max shrugged. "Do I have to?"

"Damn you, Max," he said in agitation. "It's always the same way. Everything has to go your way. Did you ever stop to think what it was like growing up as Max Decatur's little brother? Max, the strong one, the good-looking one, the bright one. Everyone liked and admired Max."

Max laughed. "Aunt Charlotte?"

Roger spat out a vulgarity. "You intimidated her. She only spoiled me because she wanted to get at you. She never loved me. Hell, she never even liked me. That was one of the reasons I jumped at the chance to take Annie away from you. I wanted to beat you just once. I knew how much you loved her. Everyone knew. It was damned near obsessive. You wouldn't let anyone near your sweet, innocent Annie." He drew in a rough breath. "Taking her away from you was the perfect revenge. Making love to *your* wife. Touching the body that you thought belonged only to *you*. It was better—"

Before Roger could finish the sentence, Max was out of the chair, and he had his brother by the throat, pulling him upright. "You bastard," Max rasped out. "You dirty, rotten bastard."

"What are you doing?"

Julia had suddenly appeared beside Max. She didn't make a move to help her husband. She simply looked slightly confused. "Roger, what's going on? You two are scaring the children."

Drawing in a deep breath, Max shifted his gaze back to his brother and realized Roger was trying to say something. Reluctantly he eased his hold on the other man's throat.

"Nothing happened," Roger said in a hoarse whisper. Reaching up, he pulled Max's hands loose and backed away from him. "Nothing happened."

"Roger," Julia said, her voice growing peevish.

Roger glanced at her, obviously distracted. "It's all right, Julia. Go on back inside and let me talk to Max."

With an impatient sound, she swung on her heels and stalked away. As soon as she was out of earshot, Max said, "What the hell do you mean 'nothing happened'?"

Roger stared at the blue water in the pool. "She came to see me about a week before we left. She said you two were having trouble. She said she wished she had never married you." Roger shrugged, still staring at the water as though a vision were unfolding there. "I told her I would take her away if that's what she wanted. I thought—Anyway a week later I picked her up at your place and we drove to Waco."

"Why Waco?"

Roger shrugged. "Why not? Neither of us had ever been there. It just seemed like a good idea at the time."

"Go on. What happened next?"

A grim smile twisted Roger's lips. "Nothing. That's what I've been trying to tell you. I got us a room at a motel. I don't have to tell you what I expected to take place in that room. But it didn't happen. When I touched her—" He broke off, and sucked air into his lungs. "When I touched her, Annie cried."

Max stared at his brother for a moment, then swung abruptly away from him. "Why?" he said, more to himself than to Roger. "Why would she do something like that? Annie never cried."

"That's just what *I* said," Roger replied, giving a short laugh. "Why in hell was she crying when it was her idea in the first place? You know what she told me? She said she was crying because I wasn't you. It was not exactly what I wanted to hear right then," Roger muttered.

Max barely heard him. He had come here to

get this thing straightened out once and for all. But nothing Roger was saying made sense. According to Roger, Annie had sought him out, rather than the other way around. The whole thing had been at her instigation.

Even if she had changed her mind at the last minute, even if she had decided she didn't want Roger after all, why would she cry for Max?"

"If she still wanted me, if she still loved me," Max said in a ragged whisper, "why did she leave? Why did she walk out on me?"

"I asked her that too. At first she wouldn't answer—she wouldn't talk to me at all—but she finally admitted she was just using me. She said she wanted to leave you and she knew your pride wouldn't let you come after her if she ran away with me." He laughed. "She apologized very prettily and, I think, sincerely. But she wouldn't tell me what was behind the whole stupid plan."

Roger shoved his hands into the pockets of his shorts and leaned back slightly. "After one miserable night," he said slowly, "which I spent in a chair in the lobby of the motel, sweating bullets, wondering if you were going to show up any minute and try to kill me, I never saw Annie again."

For a long time Max stood staring off into the distance, then he moved his shoulders wearily and turned to leave. When he had taken a few steps toward the double doors, he paused and looked back. "You said revenge was one of the reasons you ran away with Annie. What was the other reason?"

Roger reached down to pick up a newspaper. "I've loved Annie since she was ten years old," he said quietly, then he shrugged. "That's the way it goes."

Max watched his brother for a moment, then he turned and walked away.

Ten

Anne knelt on the flagstone terrace and worked the soft earth with a miniature rake. She had removed every weed, every creeping tentacle of grass, from the flower bed, but still she worked. She wasn't ready to go into the empty house. There were too many questions in the house.

It was late in the afternoon, and she had come outside as soon as Carly left. Hours ago. The sun would be going down any minute. She would have to stop then.

Today, as Anne worked, she believed she had finally discovered why gardening was so important to her. When she worked out here in the garden, she became part of something bigger. She became a part of the earth. She became a part of eternity.

Everything, all the problems big and small, that plagued every man and woman ever born, were transient things. When she was out here, she knew she was part of something more permanent, and it gave her strength.

Her newly gained wisdom didn't make her miss Max any less, but she had at least given up thoughts of using his jacket as a security blanket.

She was putting her gardening tools into a wicker basket when she heard footsteps on the flagstones. Instantly her breath caught in her throat. She didn't have to look to see who it was. She knew. Max was home.

Before she managed to get all the way to her feet, he had her in his arms, and there was laughter in his eyes as he kissed her.

Wrapping her arms around his neck, she pressed even closer. "I am *so* glad to see you," she said. "I thought you were going to call me today to let me know when you'd be back."

"I decided to tell you in person. Hey, Annie, I'm back." He hugged her, lifting her off her feet in his exuberance.

"So I see," she said, laughing with him.

"Umm, I missed you," he murmured against her neck. "You taste like the sun and the wind."

She pulled back a little so she could see his face, so she could look into his eyes. She needed to be free of the nagging little worry that had plagued her since Carly told her he was out of town.

"Where did you go?" she asked, keeping her voice carefully casual.

"I just had some business to take care of." He

raised one brow. "Do you really want to talk right now?"

The look of deep hunger in his dark eyes left her breathless. "No . . . no, I don't want to talk," she said a moment before he picked her up and threw her over his shoulder.

The caveman-style exit set the tone for their reunion. Clothes flew, and bedcovers ended in a tangle on the floor. Laughter died, and desperate need took its place.

Their lovemaking was wild and hot and fast, and the driving urgency drained her of emotion, then filled her up again. With their bodies they said what they were afraid to say with words. It was as though each was trying to fill up the empty pit the years had made in their emotional lives. But the pit refused to be filled. It took every touch, every frantic kiss, and demanded more.

An hour later she lay beside him, dazed, her eyes wide open as she stared at the ceiling. "Wow," she breathed softly.

He laughed and buried his face in her breasts. "The understatement of the year."

For a moment, for a brief flash of time, she wanted to talk to him about the urgent things they had said with their bodies. She knew what she needed—a lifetime with Max—but she wished she knew what it was that Max needed. What could she say, what could she do, that would take away the feeling that every time they touched might be the last time?

But no words that she could give him would

make the feeling go away. She had to believe that time present would wipe out time past.

"Lord, it's good to be back where I belong," he murmured against her naked flesh.

Anne closed her eyes, letting the precious words enfold her. *Thank you, God.*

"How did your meetings in Atlanta go?" Max asked.

The two of them had left the bedroom in search of food. Max sat on one side of the table, a soft drink in one hand and a roast chicken leg in the other. Anne sat on the other side with a ham sandwich.

"Lousy," she said, "but listen to this. Hector Sanchez, the man we saw in San Antonio, called Cliff yesterday. He's decided to build his new plant here."

"Hey, that's terrific. Congratulations." He bit into the chicken, chewed for a moment, then said, "When's Sanchez going to get the project started, and don't you think you'd be more comfortable over here on my lap?"

"He's flying up in a couple of days." She slid her plate across the table, then walked around and sat on his knee. "He'll meet with the council members, and if that doesn't scare the bejabbers out of him, we're set."

As she picked up her sandwich and took another bite, he said, "Just one more question."

"What's that?" she asked with her mouth full.

"Do you love me, Annie?"

When she began to cough, he pounded her on

the back. "I'm okay," she gasped weakly, wiping her watery eyes. "I'm fine . . . you can quit now."

"You don't have to answer me right away. It's just that I did some thinking while we were apart." He grinned. "Thinking's easier when you're not around. Anyway, it seems like we're building something here. At least that's the way it feels to me. You're not still afraid of me, are you? I mean, you don't think I'm still hatching revenge plots, do you?"

She stroked his face. "Truthfully? I haven't thought about it one way or the other, Max. It's been so wonderful being with you, I didn't have time to worry about it."

"Will you think about it now?"

"Okay." She squinted her eyes, concentrating fiercely, but after a moment she said, "I can't think when you're breathing on my neck . . . that's better. Actually it's not better. It's just more conducive to—"

"Think, Annie."

"Yes, sir." A second later she said, "Okay, I've thought about it, and I don't believe you're plotting revenge."

"Why?"

She frowned. "Why? You mean why do I think you're not?" When he nodded, she said, "Because before, you were always so even-tempered. That's not natural. But this time it's like you feel comfortable enough to be yourself with me. Sulky or gripy or—"

"Happy, Sneezy, or Doc," he finished dryly.

"Or sarcastic," she continued as though he

hadn't interrupted her. "And maybe it's partly because I so desperately want it to be real this time."

He rested his head against hers for a moment. "It sure feels real to me," he said, his voice deep and husky. "And that's why we have to talk again about what happened between us last time."

Her heart gave a little skip, but she kept her features even. "Last time, as in a couple of weeks ago?"

He shook his head slowly, watching her face. "Last time, as in eleven years ago."

She moistened her lips. "I thought we had done that already. What else is there to talk about?"

"Nothing specific." He grasped her shoulders and gave her a little shake. "Come on, Annie, don't tense up on me. I just want to go over some things, to clarify them in my own mind. Okay?"

"Sure," she said, and rising to her feet, she carried her plate to the sink. "You don't mind if I do the dishes while we talk? I like to stay busy."

"I've noticed that about you," he said, a smile in his voice. "I've been going over the weeks just before we split."

She exhaled a tiny puff of air. "For heaven's sake, Max, what good will that—"

"Humor me. A lot happened in those weeks. I got a new job. Almost double the salary of my old one. You and Ellie made new curtains for the apartment. They were pink because pink was the color they had on sale." He laughed. "Everywhere you looked you saw pink, pink, and more pink. Roger got a new car, a convertible. You and I went to that fancy party that McNeal and Genna gave. Neither of us had ever been in a penthouse, and I remember we joked about getting thrown out. Was it before that or after that you made the honor roll again? Did I leave anything out?"

Unable to answer, she simply shook her head and stared down at the sink.

"I think it was about a week before you left that we started fighting," he continued quietly. "I've thought about it, and for the life of me, Annie, I can't remember what those fights were about. Can you?"

Again she simply shook her head, but beneath the layer of suds her fingers clenched into tight fists.

"I don't guess it matters," he went on, "but they were bitter things. I remember that well enough."

He had moved. He stood behind her now. She didn't look at him as he picked up a dish towel and wiped her eyes, then her wet hands.

"Come sit down, honey," he said gently. He put his arm around her as he guided her out of the kitchen and into the living room.

"This is probably the third time I've ever seen you cry," he said, lowering her to the couch. Then, sitting beside her, he held both her hands between his. "The first time was at our wedding. The second time was two days before you left me. I woke up in the middle of the night, and you were sitting on the windowsill and you were crying. It scared me, Annie. You don't know how badly that scared me."

He hesitated, his gaze trained with unwavering intensity on her face. "Honey, you need to tell me what's hurting you. Let's talk about it, get it out in the open. You know as well as I do that we can't truly be together as long as there are secrets between us."

She shook her head in a helpless movement, looking away from him to stare into the empty fireplace. "I don't see why you keep—You see, Max, it can't be fixed. None of it can be changed. So why can't we just forget about it and start from here?"

"I went to see Roger."

His voice was extraordinarily calm as he dropped the bombshell in her lap.

"You did *what*? My God, Max . . . my God." She rose to her feet in agitation. "Why on earth—You keep poking around in yesterday, refusing to let it go. You've been brooding about it, fighting these bloody battles in your mind for *eleven years*, Max. But did you ever once stop to think that maybe it all worked out for the best? Take a look at who you are, at what you've accomplished. McNeal Reynolds was all set to give that job to someone else. Did you think of that? Didn't you ever once think about how lucky—"

"What are you talking about?"

She jerked her head around at the question. He was on his feet, his brow furrowed as he walked toward her.

"How did you know about that?" he asked, his

voice hoarse with confusion. "I didn't tell you anything about it."

She moistened her lips and took a nervous step backward. "After I left, I found out that you had taken the job with McNeal," she began slowly as she searched for an explanation. "And . . . and I assumed that if you hadn't taken it, he would have given it to someone else. I don't have any special knowledge. I was just—"

"You're lying, Annie."

Anger was growing in him. She could feel it. She could see it. But there was nothing she could do to stop it.

"You knew McNeal had offered me a job," he said, "and you knew I had turned it down. You knew all that *before* you left me. Now I want you to tell me how you found out."

Swinging abruptly around, she moved a step away from him. "What difference does—"

He grasped her arm and turned her back around to face him. "If it makes no difference, then why won't you tell me? You said I keep digging around in the past, that I won't let it go. Well, now's your chance to finish it once and for all. Let's have the truth, Annie. Sweet heaven, for once let's have the truth."

She stared at him, examining his face, wondering if the same dreadful tiredness weighed him down. This was it. There was one last card to turn over. And when that card was faceup, when it was revealed at last, Anne would know whether she was safe. Or bust.

Moving away from him, she returned to the couch and sat down heavily. "Genna came to see

me a couple of days after that party we went to."
Her voice was amazingly calm as she leaned her
head back against the cushion. She even managed a slight smile. "You should have seen the
way she looked at the apartment, especially all
those pink curtains. Like she was afraid poverty
was catching or something. She told me McNeal
had offered you a job and that you had turned it
down.

"You were very polite, she said. Very apprecia-
tive of the offer, but you explained that you were
married and had obligations." She gave a soft
laugh. "She made the word sound vulgar, common. And of course I knew she meant it to
sound that way, because I was the obligation,
therefore I was common. She explained that
although the job wouldn't pay much, just
your expenses, it was the opportunity of a lifetime. Remember, you called it that too. She said
there were others who would pay McNeal for the
chance to work with him. She said anyone
could see you were talented, but that even a
stupid little schoolgirl should know talent alone
wouldn't get you anywhere." She drew in a slow
breath. "Genna talked a lot that day. And she
was very convincing, Max."

"And that's it?" he asked, his voice hard, his
eyes incredulous. "Because some jealous, black-
hearted bitch tells you that you're holding me
back, you walk out on me?"

"No," she said, raising one hand to the pulse
that pounded in her temples. "Not because of
Genna. I told myself that she was wrong. I told
myself that cream always rises to the top. You

were brilliant with a camera, even back then. I was positive people would recognize that brilliance without McNeal Reynolds's help. I *believed* that, Max. Until one day about a week after Genna's visit." She raised her head and met his eyes. "You probably don't remember, but I'll never forget."

He had been late getting home from work, and by the time he arrived, Anne had finished her homework, cleaned the apartment, and had dinner on the table waiting for him. He came in the door talking about a job he had been offered, a job that offered more money, a job that required much more of his time.

Max had been so cheerful that day. Too cheerful. And as he told her what they could do with the extra money, he picked his camera up from the coffee table, and while Anne stood and watched, he had put the camera away in the bottom drawer of a worn bureau.

Every word that Genna had said came back to her then. She saw again the picture the woman had painted. A picture of Max as he gradually let his gift slip away from him while he worked to make a living. Max growing to resent her because she had stood between him and his goals. Max as an old man looking back at his life with deep regret. And Anne knew she would come to hate herself for what she had done to him, for what she had let him do to himself.

"That camera was everything to you," she whispered, her throat painfully tight as she closed her eyes against the memory. "I had to stand there and watch you put your dreams, your *life*, in a stupid bureau drawer."

Opening her eyes, she examined his stiff, pale features. "Can you remember how you were back then, Max? Can you remember how desperately you wanted to get away from Weiden Street? You said you wanted to photograph the world. Pacific islands, South American jungles, the mountains of Tibet.

"You did everything you set out to do," she said quietly. "You left Weiden Street behind and photographed all those wonderful places. You explored the world. And you did it all because *I* gave you the chance."

She stood up and took a step toward him, his continued silence giving her the courage to go on. "At seventeen maybe I wasn't wise enough to make life decisions, but even now I can't say I did the wrong thing. Because even at seventeen I loved you more than life, Max. I loved you too much to destroy your dreams. From the time I was five years old, you protected me. I decided it was my turn to protect you. Even if it was from myself."

He didn't say anything. His lips were tight and white, his hands shaking, as he turned away from her. He rested his arm on the mantel and leaned his forehead against it.

When he finally began to speak, it was in a voice so low, Anne had to move closer to hear him.

"Saint Anne," he said in a barely rasping whisper. "You made the grand sacrifice, giving up everything for the love of your man."

He swung around, his eyes blazing with a fury that was almost a physical force. "Well, *who the hell asked you to*? You damn sure didn't consult me. Why didn't I get a vote in my own freakin' future? *You had no right.*"

He clenched his shaking hands into tight fists held rigidly at his sides. "You had no right to make that kind of decision for me. I could have forgiven you for falling in love with Roger—that's not something you can control. But this? You deliberately set out to trash my life. I thought I had everything, then one day, with no warning, no explanation, I found that I had *nothing*. And you did it for me," he finished in disgust.

"You didn't come after me!" The words were out of Anne's mouth before the thought was even fully formed.

He shook his head, as though to clear it. "What?"

"You didn't come after me and ask me why." She put a hand on the back of the chair to steady herself. "You didn't follow me and take me in your arms and say let's talk about this, Annie." She drew in a ragged breath. "I told myself that I didn't want you to come after me, but it was a lie. I knew that if you found me and demanded answers, then it would be a sign. It would mean I was more important to you than your pride. More important than anything. But you didn't."

"You actually expected me to chase after you and beg you to come back?" he asked in stunned disbelief.

"No," she whispered, "I didn't expect it. By my God, I wanted it. I wanted that desperately."

"Games," he said wearily. "You were playing games with my life."

And then he turned away from her and, as she watched in helpless silence, he walked out of the room, out of the house, out of her life.

For a long time she stood absolutely still, then she pressed a hand against the stones of the fireplace, steadying herself as she slowly sat down on the hearth.

Wrapping her arms around her waist, she whispered, "You're bust, Annie."

Max had a hand on the car door when a picture rose up in his mind. He saw Annie, the way she was at seventeen. Smart and funny and shy. Incredibly strong and unconsciously vulnerable. The picture hurt. She had been a little girl, playing at being grown up. A sad, insecure little girl who had grown used to being dumped when her presence became inconvenient. A little girl who must have spent every moment worrying that someone would come along and take her happiness away from her.

You didn't come after me!

Sweet Jesus, her words had hurt him. Why hadn't he gone after her? Because he had been too much of a coward to look in her eyes when she'd told him she didn't love him anymore.

Max's cowardice had convinced her that his dreams of being a world-traveling photographer were more important to him than his sweet Annie. She had actually *believed* that.

He had always known about her deep-rooted insecurity. She had told of the times her mother had left her alone, of the times she had been shoved aside and told to keep her mouth shut. Max had known all about that. Why hadn't he spent more time showing her what she meant to him?

His only excuse was inexperience. He had simply been too young. Too young to see her needs. Too young to handle his own. And he had let them both down.

But he wasn't an inexperienced kid anymore. It was time for them to forgive each other. It was time for them to forgive themselves.

When he walked back into the house, Max stopped in the doorway and watched her rock back and forth, back and forth, her eyes wide and unseeing. She looked ill. He moved on into the room and had almost reached her before she blinked several times and turned her head toward him.

He raised both hands, palms up, in a tentative, self-mocking gesture. "I didn't make it all the way to the car," he explained slowly.

She didn't respond, but she didn't take her eyes off him as he moved across the room and knelt beside her.

"We're still a sorry pair, my Annie," he murmured, and took her in his arms.

She pressed her face against him, clutching at his arms as she began to shake violently.

"Max . . . oh God, Max," she said, and the broken whisper impaled him.

"Hush, baby, hush," he said, breathing the words against her throat. "It didn't happen. I calmed down enough to realize I was about to make the same mistake I made eleven years ago. I was about to let pride keep me from the only thing in the world that matters."

He pulled her closer, rocking her, soothing her. "I'm not going to lie to you, Annie. I don't think I'll ever get over having to spend all those years away from you. I'll always regret the things we did back then. But regret is such a silly little emotion. It can't even touch the one that made me come back in here. I love you, Annie. I always have and I always will."

She was crying now, resting her head on his shoulder as quiet tears fell. But this time Max didn't try to stop her. He knew they were tears of relief. Tears of happiness.

"You had the problem worked out wrong back then," he said as he stroked her hair. "It was never about your being a liability. It was about your lack of faith in me, in my love for you. You said you loved me more than life, but you didn't even consider the fact that I felt the same way."

When a small sound caught in her throat, he held her tighter. "Dreams of adventure and excitement, fame and fortune, those are little things, baby. Any idiot who jumps on an airplane can have that. But the kind of love we had, the kind of love we *have*, is a one-in-a-million thing. Ask any man alive, any man worthy of the name, which he'd rather have, and the answer will always be the same. He'd say, take the love. He'd say grab it with both hands and don't ever let it get away from you."

She raised her head slowly, and Max's throat closed when he saw the expression on her face. Because of all the wonders in the world, nothing could compare to the love he saw in his Annie's eyes.

In the following scene, Amy has been daydreaming while working in the vineyards, when she is distracted by her fellow grape-pickers grumbling about another worker. Fascinated by the descriptions, Amy looked up . . .

In the years that followed she would always remember that moment. She would relive it as if watching a movie inside her mind, the colors and sounds extraordinarily vivid, the dramatic impact staggering. He stood perhaps a hundred feet from them, outlined by a nearly tangible solitude, very still, studying a cluster of grapes crushed in one big fist. He was tall, with an elegant kind of brawniness to his body. Amy stared. His mystery excited her imagination.

Grape juice ran down his arm. There was weary anger in the set of his shoulders, and remnants of violence in the way he clenched the pulpy mass of burst fruit. Juice dripped onto his bare feet. His white T-shirt was stained with sweat down the center and under the arms; his baggy, wrinkled pants were an ugly green color soiled with red clay at the knees. They hung low on his hips as if about to fall off. Only a loosely knotted tie-string kept them from slipping.

He wore no hat, and his thick, charcoal-black hair was disheveled. Dark beard stubble shadowed his cheeks. His eyes were covered by unremarkable black sunglasses, but his face, making a strong, blatantly masculine profile, was anything but unremarkable.

He slung the grapes to the ground, staggering a little as he did. Then, wielding a pair of razor-sharp clippers so swiftly that Amy gasped with fear, he snipped a small cluster of grapes and shoved it into his mouth. He stripped it with one ferocious tug of his teeth then slung the empty stem over his shoulder.

"A cocky drunk, ain't he?" someone muttered.

Amy gaped at him. The others chuckled. At any second Beaucaire would come thundering down the aisle of trellises and raise hell. It would be spectacular entertainment.

What would the newcomer do next? For a man who was dirty and apparently soused, he had an aura of graceful arrogance. But then he went to a trellis post and leaned there heavily, resting his head on one arm. He no longer looked imposing. Fatigue seemed to drag at every muscle of his body. Amy clenched her hands, feeling a misfit's sympathy for another misfit but wanting to scold him for making a fool of himself.

She didn't dare. He looked dangerous—his hands were big-knuckled and dirty; ropy muscles flexed in his forearms. He wore his solitude like a shield. He swayed and stared fixedly at the ground, as if searching for a place to fall. But after a moment he dropped his clippers into a bucket and shoved himself away from the post. Staggering, he headed for a wooden crate that sat at the far end of a row. When he arrived there he disappeared around the corner.

Amy waited breathlessly for him to reappear. He didn't.

"Go get Mr. Beaucaire," someone said.

She swung toward the others. "No! I'll go see what he's doing. Don't say anything to Mr. Beaucaire. I mean it!"

Everyone stared at her. It was the first time they'd heard her speak in full sentences. She was shocked by the outburst, herself. "I, uhmmm, I b-bet he's just sick."

"Well, Lord have mercy. We finally heard Olive Oyl make more than a squeak."

Everyone chortled. Amy was mortified. Her voice humiliated her when she forgot to restrain it. People laughed at her behind her back; all through school her classmates had made fun of her. She clamped her lips together and ground her teeth as if she could crush whatever it was that made her sound the way she did. She dreaded getting a job where she had to talk. She stayed awake at night worrying about it.

But now she shoved embarrassment aside and hurried toward the crate, her heart in her throat. Behind her a woman called, "You leave that feller alone! We're gonna go get Mr. Beaucaire!"

Amy kept walking. Maybe she sympathized with all the ne'er-do-wells of the world, or maybe she was an expert on mean drunks. But she felt that there was some good reason for this man's problem.

Uncertainty pooled in her stomach. Slowing down, she crept up to the crate and stopped to listen. She heard only the rustle of grape leaves as the hot wind stroked the vineyard. Tiptoeing in the brittle grass, she sidled up to the crate's back corner and peeked around.

He lay on his back. He had removed the T-shirt and stuffed it under his head as a pillow. His hairy chest held her attention as it rose and fell in slow rhythm. His hands lay beside his head, palms up, dirty and stained with grape juice but graceful-looking nonetheless.

She stepped forward in silent awe. He slept, but there was nothing vulnerable or relaxed about his face. His mouth remained shut and firm. Above the black sunglasses a frown pulled at his brows. Up close he looked younger than she'd expected, perhaps no more than thirty.

She shifted from one foot to the other, gazing at his sleeping form in consternation. Maybe it would be best just to leave him to his fate. She bent over and sniffed. The scent of his sweat mingled with the sweet aroma of grapes, red clay, and a faint antiseptic smell that puzzled her. She knew the smell of booze and pot; neither was present.

Reassured, she knelt beside him. She removed her sunglasses and tucked them in her shirt pocket. Her hand trembling, she reached out and touched his shoulder. "Hey. Hey, wake up."

A jolt of awareness ran through him. He lifted his head and froze. She jerked her hand back. His eyes were hidden behind the glasses, but she felt as if he were scrutinizing her angrily. She fumbled with the water bottle on her belt. There was nothing else to do except blunder onward and hope he didn't yell at her.

"You gotta get up," she urged, holding the bottle toward him. "You'll get fired if you stay here. Come on, have a drink of water. You'll be okay. Get up."

When he neither moved nor replied, her nervousness gave way to exasperation. "Don't be a j-jerk! You look like you need this job! Now take a drink of water! Uhmmm, *Habla usted ingles? Si?* No? Come on, that's all the Spanish I know! Say something!"

"I would rather listen to you say something. You say quite enough for both of us, and I like your voice."

She stared at him, mesmerized. His English was excellent, but accented. The accent was not Spanish, though she couldn't identify it. His voice sank into her senses—rich, deep, beautiful. Fatigue made it hoarse, but the effect was unforgettable.

"Here," she squeaked, thrusting the water bottle close to his mouth. "This'll make you feel better."

He let his head rest on the wadded shirt again. Exhaustion creased the sides of his mouth. "Thank you, but no." He raised a hand and pushed the bottle away. "I need only to rest."

She didn't know why, but she was desperate to keep him out of trouble. He must be too tired and sick to think straight. "You're gonna get fired!"

"No, I assure you—"

"Take a sip." Amy stuck the long plastic tube between his lips and squeezed the bottle hard. He tried to swallow the jet of water and nearly strangled. Shoving the bottle away, he sat up and began coughing.

A stream of melodic non-English purled from his throat, and she didn't have to understand it to know that he was disgusted. She clutched the water bottle to her chest.

As he finished he whipped his glasses off and turned a stern gaze on her. Dread filled her chest, but she was too stunned to do anything except stare back. No one would call him pretty; in fact, his nose was blunt and crooked, his cheekbones jagged, and his mouth almost too masculine. It was a tough Bogart mouth, and the effect was heightened by a thin white scar that started an inch below his bottom lip and disappeared under his chin.

But all that made him handsome in a way she'd never encountered before. And his eyes, large and darkly lashed in the tough face, seemed to have been inherited from a different, more elegant heritage.

"Are you . . . you're not one of the regular workers," she said in confusion.

"No."

"Are you sick or something?"

"Or something." His expression was pensive for a moment. "I am only tried . . . just tired . . . It will pass."

"Oh. Okay. Sorry to pester you." She started to rise. He clasped her arm.

"Don't leave. I didn't mean to chase you away. Here. Give me the water. Perhaps you're right. It helps."

While she watched in amazement he drank slowly from the bottle. She spent an awkward moment gazing at the silky movement of muscles in his neck and chest. He lowered the bottle and studied her some more. The skin around his lips was tight and pale. He blinked in groggy thought, then handed the bottle back. "You make me feel remarkably better. *Merci.*" His mouth curved in a private, off-center smile that erased all sternness from his face.

Amy caught her breath. Her shyness returned like a smothering blanket. *Merci*. He was *French*. Maurice Chevalier. The Eiffel Tower. Paris. Tongue kissing. "Don't pass out, okay? Bye."

CIRCLE OF PEARLS
by Rosalind Laker

When Julia Palliser was born one October day in 1641, a rare and beautiful Elizabeth drop-pearl was placed in her tiny palm. It symbolized the only remaining gown of Elizabeth I's extensive wardrobe—a pearl-encrusted gift from Julia's grandmother, a legacy binding three generations of women.

All her life she has loved Christopher Wren, the brilliant mathematican and architect who would one day help to rebuild London. Why then is she irresistibly drawn to Adam Warrender, the enemy her stepfather wants her to marry?

In the following scene, Julia weds the man she never dreamed of loving . . .

Certain moments stood out in her mind afterwards. The gold ring sliding onto her finger. The surprising tenderness of Adam's kiss in the vestry before they signed the register there and the fragrance of her Sotherleigh posy when Mary, who had held it for her during the service, handed it back to her. Then walking down the aisle with her fingers on Adam's wrist while everyone smiled and nodded and the organ made the air tremble. Among the sea of faces only Christopher's stood out, but she did not allow herself to meet his eyes. This was Adam's day and in the compromise she had arranged with herself she could not fail him in what was rightfully his. Her golden shoes bore her on her way out into the sunshine with the man she had married.

It was a light-hearted ride home and from the village onwards there were petals in the path of the coach. Near the gates she and Adam threw showers of silver coins and were cheered and applauded right to the door of Sotherleigh.

Sotherleigh had not seen such feasting and merriment for many years. Wine flowed and dish after dish was borne in to replenish the long table in the Great Hall and the extra tables that had been added. Speeches were made and toasts drunk while musicians played in the gallery, sometimes barely to be heard above the chatter and the laughter. In a meadow that lay the same distance from both Sotherleigh and Warrender half an ox was being roasted, and mutton turned on spits as the tenants of both estates celebrated the marriage, barrels set up to supply them with all the ale they could drink.

Adam and Julia led their guests into the dancing in an adjoining room. When Michael partnered her they exchanged a glance as the measure took them past the Queen's Door.

"If only I had known," she said on a sigh, referring obliquely to their talk at breakfast.

"Hush," he replied with a slight shake of his head. "Think no more about it. This is a time for rejoicing, not for regrets."

She was not entirely sure about that, but then he did not know of the emotional turmoil she had been through and which was not yet over. Fortunately it was proving easy to enjoy herself. Even with Christopher as she whirled in a country dance, her merriment was spontaneous and her laughter full of delight. He had heard that he was to be appointed the Savilian professor of Astronomy at Oxford, the most tremendous honor to be bestowed on a man as young as he.

"You're turning upside down the custom of having grey-beards in high places," she declared teasingly.

"It will be a few months before I take up the appointment and maybe I'll have turned grey myself by then," he joked, holding her hand high as she danced under his arm.

"You'll always be young, even when you're old in years," she insisted, half seriously and half in jest.

"How can you be sure of that?" he asked in the same vein.

"In this gown and my golden slippers I can be sure of anything today." Playfully she kissed the tip of her finger and placed it against his mouth. Then the shifting pattern of the dance swept her away as another partner claimed her and he continued the measure with Anne, who skipped light as a feather.

Time, speeding by, brought the supper hour when every guest found the traditional gift by the places set at the tables. There were elaborately cuffed and scented gauntlets for the men and white kid gloves perfumed with a floral fragrance for the women. Again the feasting was prolonged, noisy singing increasing among those getting drunker than the rest.

Julia, chatting to those sitting opposite her at the head table, failed to notice when the singers were hushed and an amused and expectant silence began to fall on the jovial company. Every head was turned in her direction. With a start she saw that Susan and Mary and Faith had come to her chair. It was time for her to be escorted upstairs by her ladies. A blush flared into her face and then she recovered herself. As she rose from her chair Adam, sitting beside her, was the first on his feet and the whole assembly followed suit. With dignity she acknowledged the cheers and raised glasses as she began to proceed from the Great Hall.

In the bedchamber of the apartment that had been Katherine's, Julia was suddenly assailed by a rush of panic as Mary began to unlace the back of her gown. Sarah, assisted by Molly, had spread the linen sheet on which Julia stood to prevent the Elizabethan gown from coming in contact with the floor when it fell about her feet. But she was reluctant to disrobe. She had not minded when Susan had removed the coronet of roses, faded now, from her head or when the pearl ear-bobs and the necklet had been replaced in the silver casket held by Faith, but the gown was another matter. It had sustained her throughout the day, given her a light heart when otherwise her earlier melancholy could have stayed unrelentingly with her.

She crossed her arms and held the gown by the sleeves as the released lacing at the back caused it to slip down from her shoulders. She wondered what these five women in the room would say if she said she would not care how she was ravished in the night if she could keep this gown on her body.

"Step out of your gown now," Susan said quite firmly, seeing that she delayed. "It will not be long before Adam is escorted here."

Julia obeyed and felt the gown slip from her like a farewell caress, leaving her vulnerable and armorless. Sarah picked it up while Molly gathered up the discarded petticoats and stockings, removing them with the sheet after they had both bobbed to the bride and wished her a good night. Faith helped Julia into her nightgown.

"What a pretty garment this is!" Faith, modest to the extreme, thought such a soft cambric would be too revealing for her own choice, for the lace frill at the scooped neckline fell so low it almost revealed Julia's nipples, which could be clearly discerned. "Did you sew it yourself?"

"No, Mary did," Julia answered absently, sitting down before the mirror at her toilet table. "I've been too busy dealing in ribbons."

Faith was amazed. How could any girl be too busy to sew her own bridal nightgown? She had not realised quite how seriously Julia was taking her ribbon business.

Mary had finished brushing Julia's hair from its coiffure into the curls that danced down her back. Then it was Susan who saw her into bed and brought the sheet up over her breasts for concealment as she sat up against her pillows. From the distance there came a rising tumult of drunken voices raised in lewd songs and bursts of cheering.

"The bridegroom is on his way," Susan announced, glancing about the room to make sure that all was in order. The approaching din grew louder.

"Don't let all those people in!" Julia appealed urgently.

Susan nodded and guided Faith and Mary out into the parlour beyond where they formed a phalanx in front of the bedchamber door. It was to no avail. As the crowd of young men swarmed through into the apartment, all the older ones and the ladies remaining downstairs, the first to reach the three women simply picked them up with battle yells and, ignoring their protests, carried them forward into the bedchamber where they were set down on their feet again.

She looked for Adam and could not see him. Then there came a ripple through the gathering as those who had not yet managed to get into the bedchamber helped Michael and the groomsman push Adam through the jam in the doorway. For a few minutes he was wedged with the rest and then he was seized to be shoved and jostled towards the bed, people well-meaning but rough in their eagerness. He reached the foot in a dishevelled state with his dressing-robe torn and his nightshirt ripped from one shoulder. Leaning a hand against the carved bedpost, his grin was resigned as he recovered his breath.

Turning to Julia, Adam cupped the back of her head in his

hand and she tipped helplessly against him as he kissed her long and hard. The raucous approbation might have brought down a ceiling less well constructed than that of the Sotherleigh bedchamber. Still holding her head when the kiss ended, he put his cheek against hers and whispered in her ear. "That is what they wanted to see. Now they will go."

He was right. At last Susan was able to be in command again with Michael to assist her, although even then it took time before they were able to shepherd the last merry-maker out of the apartment back to the celebrations downstairs.

"Mary! Wait a moment!"

As Mary paused, surprised, Julia sprang from the bed to take up her bridal posy, which had been placed in a vase of water on a table. Careless of the drops spattering her nightgown, she rushed with it to Mary and put it into her hands.

"May you know joy in time to come!"

Mary's eyes filled with tears. Too choked to speak, she hugged Julia in gratitude and hurried away, forgetting to close the door. Slowly Julia pushed it shut. Then she stiffened. Without turning she knew that Adam had left the bed and was coming soundlessly towards her on his bare feet.

"That posy was well given, Julia."

Still she did not turn. "She is in love with my brother."

"I know."

"How?"

"She talks about him with shining eyes at the least excuse."

"Such is the weakness of lovers."

"Not with all, or else I should have shouted my love of you from the pinnacles of Westminster." He drew aside the curtain of her hair to place a kiss on the nape of her neck. Moving his hand down to her waist, he gently swivelled her round to face him and then kissed her, loving her mouth. To his joy her arms slid by her volition round his neck and he held her close, a new harmony created between them by the natural hunger of their young and healthy bodies, the fierce magnetism that had long been between them and his love that sought to find an answering chord in her.

When their kiss ended she laid her head against his shoulder. "I'm sure our marriage mended many feuds today."

He stroked one hand down her back. "There were new beginnings for quite a few people and especially for us."

"I think ours began when I put on my Elizabethan gown this morning. All day I saw it as the safeguard of happiness, a talisman without which everything would fade away again. It made me reluctant to discard it when my ladies brought me up here, but I need not have feared. What it ignited is still with me."

"Maybe it's because I have taken over its charge to be the protector of that happiness."

She raised her head and they looked deep into each other's eyes. "I want more than anything that we should fulfil each other's lives, no matter what is against us," she said quietly.

"There is nothing that we can't defeat together."

He kissed her again and she clung to him, hoping his words would prove true, for if their marriage failed to reach the heights the fault would be hers, of that she was sure. She wanted an end to being torn apart and for the compromise she had made to be a bridge to this man, although if it would take years or a lifetime she could not estimate. Love could not be driven out, but had to take its own time. Not even a new love had the power to banish the old completely if a wilful heart stood its ground.

"Take me to bed," she whispered. . . .

FOREVER
by Theresa Weir

New Fanfare author Theresa Weir will touch your hearts with FOREVER, a beautiful and passionate love story between two people who learn to live—and love—again. When journalist Sammy Thoreau loses much of his memory in a devastating car accident, doctors pronounce him a lost cause until Dr. Rachel Collins bravely takes on his case. But she doesn't expect Sammy, with his glittering dark eyes and sexy smile, to reverse their roles with a vengeance, to expose the secret pain she tries to hide, and to ignite forbidden emotions. . . .

In the following excerpt, Rachel lays eyes on her newest patient for the first time.

The majority of Rachel's cases were outpatients. A few were

sometimes hospitalized for short stays, but it had been over three years since she'd taken on anyone who might require long-term, intensive therapy, the kind that could be so emotionally draining. She hoped she was ready for it.

When she reached Samuel Thoreau's room, Rachel's first reaction was of indignation.

He was lying on his back on the bed. Even though he appeared to be totally sedated, his wrists were secured to the side rails, and he was wearing a green hospital gown with the word *Psycho* stenciled across the front in three-inch black letters.

"He arrived like this," the floor nurse whispered. "I got his blood pressure, but when I tried to take his temperature his teeth clamped down so hard on the thermometer I was afraid it might break off in his mouth. I wasn't sure what to do with him. . . ."

"We'll begin without restraints—harmless until proven otherwise."

"But Dr. Fontana said—"

"Mr. Thoreau is my patient, not Dr. Fontana's."

She approached the bed. The man's scalp was covered with a new crop of hair that was as inky black as his eyebrows. His face was hollow-cheeked and yellow-tinged—jaundiced, most likely from overmedication. He needed a shave and a bath and clean hospital clothes.

"Mr. Thoreau," she said softly, "I am Dr. Collins."

In a head injury case, the patient could appear to be totally incoherent when in actuality he wasn't. Rachel was always careful to guard her words, to not say anything that might cause undue distress.

"You're here at the University Hospital in La Grange, Iowa, because you were in an accident and hurt your head. I'm going to be helping to take care of you."

She watched his gaunt face for any sign of response and was rewarded with a slight movement beneath his closed lids.

"First of all, I'm going to make you more comfortable by untying your hands." She untied one, then the other. His arms fell limply to the bed.

She felt the pulse on his wrist. It was slow due to the overload of drugs in his system. Then she examined the area at the base of his skull, finding a small red ridge of scar tissue. No sign of infection. A miracle. He'd healed despite everything.

Rachel was about to call the nurse aside with further instructions when the man's eyelids twitched, then opened.

She found herself being regarded by a pair of coal-black eyes set deeply in bruised sockets. The look in them made her want to cry. Empty. Expecting nothing. Wanting nothing.

Once again, anger burned in her. How could anyone treat a patient this way? They had violated one of the important rules of medicine: First, do no harm. Apparently some institutions were still the stuff bad dreams were made of.

And then Samuel Thoreau did something that made her go weak with self-doubt, made her wonder if she'd just been fooling herself, made her fear that she might no longer have the emotional strength needed to survive this kind of journey, a journey that could take her deep into his psyche.

With defeated eyes, Samuel Thoreau looked up at her and whispered through dry lips, "I'll . . . be . . . good."

Several weeks later

It was Sunday morning. Rachel didn't usually stop at the hospital on Sundays, but she wanted to check on Sammy. He had been moved to a long-term facility, which meant he was in a larger room that was more like living quarters.

It was there that Rachel found him pacing back and forth.

As soon as her footfall sounded in the doorway, he swung around. The second he realized who it was, his frown turned to a smile. "Dr. Collins!" He bounded across the room, his energy buffeting her like a gust of ocean wind.

"I have a great idea. Let's go somewhere. Blow this hole for a while. What do you say?"

Restless, pent-up energy met bewildered sorrow. It took Rachel a moment to gather her thoughts.

"I could leave here for a while, couldn't I? Just an hour or two?"

The irrational side of her wanted to say yes. But the practical doctor knew he was too unpredictable, his psyche still too raw.

"Sammy . . . you're not quite ready. Maybe next week . . ."

"Next week!" He raked his fingers across his scalp, making his bristly hair stand on end. "I've got to get out of here," Sammy said, his voice edged with panic. "Just for a while. For an hour. A few minutes. I need to breathe."

His gaze shifted around the room, seeking a solution, seeking an escape, finally coming to light on her once more. "I'll be good, I swear." He drew a finger across his chest. "Cross my heart."

The desperation in his eyes was almost her undoing. What he was suggesting wasn't all that irregular. It was only a matter of signing a pass. But he wasn't ready. *She* wasn't ready.

He was watching her closely, the way he always did.

"You're not going to let me go, are you?" he asked.

"Sammy—"

"Don't say it. You don't have to say it. I can tell by your face."

He was moving toward her, closing the space between them. She took one step back, then another, until she was pressed to the wall with nowhere to run. And he was still coming.

"You're afraid," he stated. "What are you afraid of, Rachel?"

"Nothing."

"Tell me the truth. You're afraid of me, aren't you?"

"No."

"Yes. I've seen it in your face before, I can see it in your face now. Sometimes you look up from that clipboard of yours and catch me staring. And I can tell it bothers you. Why does it bother you, Rachel?" When she didn't answer, he asked, "Do you ever wonder what I'm thinking when I'm watching you?"

She swallowed.

"Want to know?"

She shook her head.

"No? But you're a shrink. You're supposed to want to hear my deepest, darkest secrets. Isn't that right? My deepest, darkest desires."

His voice was rough, threatening . . . and, heaven help her, sensual.

She brought up her hand. Fingers splayed, she pressed against his chest, trying to hold him back . . . but he didn't move. She knew she could scream for help and someone would come. But she also knew Sammy would never hurt her. At least not physically. But his words . . . they were a different thing altogether.

"Sometimes when I look at you," Sammy whispered, his face only inches from her, "I get horny. Did you know that, *Doctor* Collins?"

"Sammy." Once again she shoved the solidness of his chest, but it was like shoving something set in concrete.

"You know what else?" he asked slowly, thoughtfully. "A lot of times I wonder what it would be like to . . . *kiss* you."

From his emphasis on the word *kiss*, she knew he was insinuating much more than a kiss.

She felt her own panic wind higher. This had to stop. Immediately. "I'm your doctor. You're my patient. There can be nothing sexual between us."

"So *you* say."

"So the physician's rules of ethics say."

"Screw the rules. Screw ethics." His voice dropped, became more intimate. "Tell me, Rachel. How long's it been since you were . . . *kissed*?"

That inflection again. And now he pressed his body firmly against hers so they were touching from chest to knee.

His head came down, his mouth drawing nearer. . . .

THE EDITOR'S CORNER

With the six marvelous **LOVESWEPT**s coming your way next month, it certainly will be the season to be jolly. Reading the best romances from the finest authors—what better way to enter into the holiday spirit?

Leading our fabulous lineup is the ever-popular Fayrene Preston with **SATAN'S ANGEL**, LOVESWEPT #510. Nicholas Santini awakes after a car crash and thinks he's died and gone to heaven—why else would a beautiful angel be at his side? But Angel Smith is a flesh-and-blood woman who makes him burn with a desire that lets him know he's very much alive. Angel's determined to work a miracle on this magnificent man, to drive away the pain—and the peril—that torments him. A truly wonderful story, written with sizzling sensuality and poignant emotions—one of Fayrene's best!

How appropriate that Gail Douglas's newest LOVESWEPT is titled **AFTER HOURS**, #511, for that's when things heat up between Casey McIntyre and Alex McLean. Alex puts his business—and heart—on the line when he works *very* closely with Casey to save his newspaper. He's been betrayed before, but Casey inspires trust . . . and brings him to a fever pitch of sensual excitement. She never takes orders from anyone, yet she can't seem to deny Alex's passionate demands. A terrific book, from start to finish.

Sandra Chastain weaves her magical touch in **THE-JUDGE AND THE GYPSY**, LOVESWEPT #512. When Judge Rasch Webber unknowingly shatters her father's dream, Savannah Ramey vows a Gypsy's revenge: She would tantalize him beyond reason, awakening longings he's denied, then steal what he most loves. She couldn't know she'd be entangled in a web of desire, drawn to the velvet caress of Rasch's voice and the ecstatic fulfillment in his arms. You'll be thoroughly enchanted with this story of forbidden love.

The combination of love and laughter makes **MIDNIGHT KISS** by Marcia Evanick, LOVESWEPT #513, completely irresistible. To Autumn O'Neil, Thane Clayborne is a sexy stick-in-the-mud, and she delights in making him lose control. True, running a little wild is not Thane's style, but Autumn's seductive beauty tempts him to let go. Still, she's afraid that the man who bravely sacrificed a dream for another's happiness could never care for a woman who ran scared when it counted most. Another winner from Marcia Evanick!

With his tight jeans, biker boots, and heartbreak-blue eyes, Michael Hayward is a **TEMPTATION FROM THE PAST**, LOVESWEPT #514, by Cindy Gerard. January Stewart has never seen a sexier man, but she knows he's more trouble that she can handle. Intrigued by the dedicated lawyer, Michael wants to thaw January's cool demeanor and light her fire. Is he the one who would break down her defenses and cast away her secret pain? Your heart will be stirred by this touching story.

A fitting final course is **JUST DESSERTS** by Theresa Gladden, LOVESWEPT #515. Caitlin MacKenzie has had it with being teased by her new housemate, Drew Daniels, and she retaliates with a cream pie in his face! Pleased that serious Caitie has a sense of humor to match her lovely self, Drew begins an ardent pursuit. She would fit so perfectly in the future he's mapped out, but Catie has dreams of her own, dreams that could cost her what she has grown to treasure. A sweet and sexy romance—what more could anybody want?

FANFARE presents four truly spectacular books this month! Don't miss bestselling Amanda Quick's **RENDEZ-VOUS**. From London's most exclusive club to an imposing country manor, comes this provocative tale about a free-thinking beauty, a reckless charmer, and a love that defied all logic. **MIRACLE**, by beloved LOVESWEPT author Deborah Smith, is the unforgettable contemporary romance of passion and the collision of worlds, where a man and a woman who couldn't have been more different learn that love may be improbable, but never impossible.

Immensely talented Rosalind Laker delivers the exquisite historical **CIRCLE OF PEARLS**. In England during the days of plague and fire, Julia Pallister's greatest test comes from an unexpected quarter—the man she calls enemy, a man who will stop at nothing to win her heart. And in **FOREVER**, by critically acclaimed Theresa Weir, we witness the true power of love. Sammy Thoreau had been pronounced a lost cause, but from the moment Dr. Rachel Collins lays eyes on him, she knows she would do anything to help the bad-boy journalist learn to live again.

Happy reading!

With every good wish for a holiday filled with the best things in life,

Nita Taublib

Nita Taublib
Associate Publisher/LOVESWEPT
Publishing Associate/FANFARE

Miracle

by

Deborah Smith

An unforgettable story of love and the collision of two worlds. From a shanty in the
Georgia hills to a television studio in L.A.,
from the heat and dust of Africa to glittering
Paris nights -- with warm, humorous, passionate characters, MIRACLE weaves a spell
in which love may be improbable but never
impossible.